The Malady of Love

Sierra Ernesto Xavier

Grosvenor House
Publishing Limited

This book is published by
Grosvenor House Publishing Ltd
Link House
140 The Broadway, Tolworth, Surrey, KT6 7HT.
www.grosvenorhousepublishing.co.uk

A CIP record for this book
is available from the British Library

ISBN 978-1-80381-031-7

CONTENTS

v

Introduction

I have from the outset tried to change the reader's experience or perspective on what is being read; a bold undertaking, but something which has some logic to it. Most books follow the format of description, description, description about the time, the place and the person. Every aspect of the mood, environment and atmosphere is spoon-fed to the reader; the greater the spoon-feeding, the greater our applause. I started *The Malady of Love* (*Malady* henceforth) with the intention of having no references to time, place or person, amongst other things: a dialogue-only story between two characters.

In arenas such as the therapeutic relationship, clients talk about the issues availing their 'story' or 'narrative' to the therapist. Whilst the physical aspects (i.e. the people, the places and the times) differ, there are similarities between clients in their emotional narratives: two people may experience different 'physical' elements of bereavement but the same anger, guilt, rage, etc. remain common. We can all understand the experience of these emotions without reference to any other description.

Furthermore, in leaving *Malady* as pure dialogue, I hope to offer the reader a relationship to 'what' is being said, both in terms of the psychological and emotional, and not the context (i.e. the physical environment) it is said in. For books that describe Africa remain in Africa by their ambience. Books that use names fix these names to a particular country — a French man reading a Russian name will know that the language of the name is one step removed from him. Indeed, this same alienation can be applied to the description of characters. I would thus like the reader to fill in their own elements and focus on the 'what' that is being said.

True portability can never be attained as the language that is used today will be outdated tomorrow. As such, I have attempted to create some sort of artifice in the dialogue, to allow the reader to follow some pattern or rhythm. By doing this, the reader is removed from comparing their own pattern of thought, as this falsehood or artifice is shared by all.

It is clear from reading *Malady* that repetition is the major stylistic device used. Refer yourself to clients in therapy. Often, whilst trying to express themselves, clients are thinking and being emotive at the same time. When cognition and emotion affect one another, the client may need repeated attempts to clarify what is going on for him inside. Their first attempt may not be as entirely accurate as they wish it to be and neither may their second, but the second may describe the first slightly differently and be more aligned to what they want.

'It is as if I cannot be with someone… As if I am not allowed to be with someone.'

Indeed, any declaration of emotion with uncertainty might be expressed with multiple attempts, each trying to convey a more accurate meaning to the listener:

'You hurt me. You hurt me in a way I did not think possible. You hurt me over something which seemed so small.'

I carry on this repetition extensively throughout the story, although I would like to assert that the emphasis here is on the 'confessional' element and not on the two characters having had or being in therapy.

Because I have elected to use this self-declarative emotional style for both characters and have left the tone of their voices the same, I have placed the female voice in *italics*, to help differentiate the two. Ideally the single point of differentiation I wanted was to be in the 'what' that was being said between the characters: one person's story being different from another's. However, this might have become too difficult to follow as a character in a later chapter may reference a sentence that was said in an earlier one. Without a change in the tone of their voice, an enormous burden is placed on the reader.

The only sense of time are references to what has been said previously (for it to be referenced at point B it must have been said prior to it, at point A), hopefully creating a forward chronology of events. I have occasionally referred to time as well ('it has been three years *since*').

I hope the reader will look at *Malady* as a different kind of venture from a writer in development.

Sierra Ernesto Xavier, 2009.

ix

Maladie

I

Our Meeting

You hurt me. You hurt me in a way that I did not think possible. You hurt me over something which seemed so small; over something which seemed so simple. But it is the impact of this small simple thing that I remember. Even though we only met once and we did not really know one another, it felt as if you had rejected me. And by rejecting me you hurt me. I remember that. I remember the way I felt hurt.

I think you are mistaken. Mistaken in believing that something I did hurt you; mistaken that it was I who caused the hurt that you feel. You say you remember it. You say you remember the hurt. Do you remember that small simple thing that you did? It was you who hurt me. It was I who felt rejected. I did not reject you. I thought we got on well together. After all, when we met that day, we shared many conversations, many smiles, many thoughts —

Yes, we did. We shared many things. We shared conversations. We shared our smiles, our thoughts, our feelings — and emotions. Yes, we shared our feelings. That is why it was important to me. That is why I do not understand why you hurt me.

It was important to me, also. It was important to me to have known your thoughts, to have known your feelings, to have seen your smiles. It was important to me and that is why it was painful, painful to know that the small simple thing that you did had hurt me.

I still remember your words. I still remember your smiles.

I remember. I remember I liked you. I remember that.

But there are some things I do not understand. There are some things that are not clear to me. Why did you hurt me? Why did you not respond?

Respond? Respond? I corresponded shortly after we met... We talked about this, we talked about that, we exchanged pleasantries, but we never discussed 'us'. We never discussed our meeting.

4

Yes, that's right, you did. You did contact me. We did talk. We talked about this and we talked about that. But why do you call it 'our meeting'? Is that what it was to you, is that what it meant to you — 'Our Meeting' — a meeting?

No… Sometimes it is easier to say 'Our Meeting'. It is easier for me to say that than what it actually was. It is easier to say 'Our Meeting' than 'a date'. It is easier because of the hurt I feel. Because… Because I invested my time, my self, my thoughts, my feelings. Yes, my feelings. To say it was a date, which came to nothing, is like saying that my words… my thoughts and feelings… my actions, my – myself came to nothing.

But why did you not tell me this when you contacted me?

I could not tell you. I could not say anything. I was waiting. Waiting for you. Waiting for you to mention 'us'. Waiting for you to mention our… 'meeting'.

You were waiting? For me?... I thought you did not want to discuss it. I thought that <u>you</u> did not want to discuss 'us'. I thought that was why you did not want to raise the matter. I listened... and I waited. I waited for you to say something. I waited for some kind of signal, some kind of sign – something to let me know.

No. *You* did not mention it. You did not mention it and *you* did not ask a question relating to it. *As a woman*, if that had meant anything to you, then *you* would have asked.

<u>*As a woman*</u>, *I was leaving it up to you.*

I thought that you might not have liked something I had said. That you had not liked something I had done, that you did not like me. That somehow I had offended you.

No.

That there was something wrong with me.

No, no.

That there was something about my very being that you did not like.

No, no... Yes, I can see... 'Our Meeting'.

No, there is nothing wrong with you. I wanted you to say something. I wanted to hear that you liked me. I wanted to hear that you wanted to be with me.

I do... I do. I wanted to say something. I wanted to tell you. I wanted to tell you all those things. But sometimes when I want to say something — I cannot. Sometimes, when I want to say something, I need to feel safe before I can say it.

You need to feel safe? Do I make you feel unsafe?

No... It is not you that makes me feel unsafe. It is a fear that

I have — a fear that I have always had.

Fear?

Ever since I was a child… Ever since I can remember, I do not know how it started but it has been there… Always.

Before… It would happen all the time. It would happen for everything. It would happen for whatever reason… at any time… It would just happen.

It is there… I do not know why it comes… It comes only at times… but it is there reminding me… reminding me that what I want to do or what I want to say cannot be done or said.

It prevents me… prevents me from doing something… prevents me from saying something… stopping me… halting me in my life… halting me living a life.

Now… it still happens… It happens less… But it still happens many times.

Here… in a situation like this, it happens… It happens when… when I… I want to be with someone… When I like someone… When I want to be with… to be with a woman.

So many times it has occurred. So many times have I been left with this fear. It consumes me.

It is just there... preventing me from doing things... preventing me from being with someone... Preventing me from being with women.

Yet, I know many women. They are my friends. When they are my friends, it is all okay. When, with some women, I want them to be something more... more than just a friend — that is when it happens — that moment in which I think about them differently... the moment I think about being with somebody... that moment I wish to fill my loneliness.

It is as if I cannot be with someone... as if I am not allowed to be with someone... as if I am not allowed to be happy.

So many times have I felt something for someone, so many times have I done nothing, so many times have I lost opportunities.

I know what I want and I can feel it in my heart. I can feel the emotions in my heart. I can feel them rising. They excite me. They fill me. They fill my void.

In that moment, I know I have the ability to say it. In that moment, I have the desire to say it. But when my desire and my ability meet, it is then that it happens. It is then that my voice remains paralysed. It is then that I remain paralysed.

I can feel my breath carrying the words. I can feel my desire wanting to speak. Yet it all remains in a shapeless form: my voice box freezes... My body becomes frozen.

I can feel my breath escaping me. I can feel my breath carrying the wordless words... I can feel it carry the voiceless voice. Everything in my mind wants to say something; everything in my body is unable to say it. In that moment, in that instant, I cast my eyes and head down to one side, knowing I have lost the opportunity... as I have lost the silent breath that escapes me.

It is as if what I want I cannot have. It is as if I cannot have the truth I desire, as if I fear the truth. That truth is to be feared. That 'being with someone' is to be feared. That what I want is to be feared.

I have wanted to ask, I have wanted to. I have seen the words come from within me. I have felt them escaping from within, whilst I remain paralysed. I see those words floating in this space around us. Those words, these words, the words — they are lonely. They are lost...

I, too, at times, do not like calling it a 'date'. I, too, am afraid... Afraid for other reasons... afraid of loneliness... afraid of being alone.

I have met many people before, been on many dates — dates which I feel I had to go on. I do it because I am lonely, because I do not want to be lonely. Perhaps I want to avoid the loneliness of my existence, to occupy myself, to take my mind off things, so that I can feel alive.

Sometimes my sister reminds me of my loneliness. She reminds me of what it may be like not to be with someone.

She is no longer with me. I have lost her. She has passed away. But she keeps reaching out to me, reminding me of my loneliness. Perhaps that is what I am looking for: someone to comfort me, someone to hold me, someone to take away my sister from my mind. There were not enough times for her to need me. Not enough times for her to want me. I do not remember her arms ever being around me.

I know, really, that the loneliness cannot be down to her. It is up to me; it is my sense of loneliness. It is my need to feel alive, my need to be touched, perhaps my need to be held. I would like to be held, but held as a woman. I want to feel like a woman.

When I wake up... When I open my eyes and I do not see anyone lying next to me, I do things to avoid that moment, to avoid that emptiness. To avoid that moment in which I wake up and realise that nobody is there.

It is difficult at times to know there is no one to hold you, that there is no one to touch you, to not to have the feeling of a warm body near you. It is difficult at times to know that your desires cannot be satisfied.

I am not sure, but maybe I try to look for someone because I do not want to know that there are no arms to hold me... that there are no hands to touch me... that there is no warmth around me... no warmth in my bed.

I also do not want to feel that my desires are not important... that I am not important... that <u>they</u> are insignificant... that <u>I</u> am insignificant. I do not want to feel that I can only exist without these layers of feelings, these sensitivities, these intimacies.

But deep down, I am afraid that at the very core of my existence I am lonely: that I only exist without these sentiments; that I exist without others. To know that someone has not chosen me, to know someone may not think enough of me, that someone may not value me... that I am not valued.

Perhaps my need to be with others is because I want to be valued, to know, to some degree, that someone wants me. To know someone wants me in that instant when I wake up and look beside me.

I seek others because I... I... I need to know that I am attractive to someone. I need to know somebody likes me, that they like me for that instant — that instant when I wake up and open my eyes and do not see anyone next to me.

Sometimes I also need to feel like a woman, to know that I am a woman. That my femininity can express itself, that <u>it</u> can be acknowledged, that <u>I</u> can be acknowledged as being feminine, as being a woman.

Perhaps I date because my self-esteem needs to know that I am of value to someone... that I need to exist with and for others... that without others I do not exist, that without others I am alone.

It is strange... In some way, we seem to be tied together by words:

with you, it is your difficulty in saying them; with me, it is my need to say them. You cannot say words because of a fear; I can say words because of my need to avoid loneliness.

Yes, yes, I can see how these words may tie us together. Perhaps these words that we share can build a bridge between my fear and your loneliness. I would like that. I would like that very much. It would be nice to overcome this fear I have with you. Perhaps you would let me help you overcome the loneliness that you feel and let you know that there is someone else besides your sister who can be there for you.

I like you. I would like to get to know you. I would like us to be together, to get to know one another. Would you like that? Would you like to get to know me?

Do you remember the hurt that I felt? Do you remember that I felt rejected? I think I felt that way because of what happened when we met: we shared many conversations, many smiles and many thoughts. It is those feelings that tell me that I like you, that I liked you from the beginning.

I would like to go out with you, to get to know you. But it may take time, time to trust one another, time to form that bridge with our words. I would like us to try. I would like to see if we can be together.

13

II

Distance in My Eyes

I remember. I remember when we first started to go out with one another. I recollect that you said that you have always wanted to 'be with someone', that you have always wanted to 'be' with a woman. I think you said that in the moment you feel something for someone, the moment you feel something for a woman, that you somehow freeze, that somehow you maintain loneliness because of a fear you have. You have been bold enough to see me a few times, you have been bold enough to 'meet' with me, but to me that is what they remain − meetings. It is as if you are here and yet not here. It is as if you are not fully 'present' with me: sometimes you can be, sometimes you are not; it gets so confusing.

I have tried to get close to you. I thought we had gone past that stage in our relationship, the stage of introduction. Even though we have only met a few times, I had hoped that we had gone past that point where we are acting in front of one another, the point when we are trying to sell ourselves − that part in a relationship when we want to show ourselves in a positive light, when we try to be on our best behaviour.

I had hoped, with what we had discussed in our time together, that you would have realised that we can move our relationship forward. I thought you might also have been aware by now that I am not to be feared. That you might have seen there is nothing to fear. In many ways, I am like you — emotional in my needs. Maybe it is this that has changed your mind.

Maybe... maybe... you want the words to remain lost in the space around us. I would like to know if this space is filled with those silent words. I would like to know if I have not given you a sense that those silent words can be safe around me. Perhaps it is this space between us that you do not want to enter. Perhaps I do not provide enough security to make you want to be fully 'present' with me.

No, no. I have not changed my mind and, yes, we have only met a few times, but I do want to be with you. I do want to close this space that is between us. I have been trying to do this. I have been trying to make the words that I say louder. I have been trying to make the deeds that I do much clearer. It is not you who are preventing me from being fully 'present' with you. It is me. It is something here inside me that I battle with.

There are things that are difficult for me. There are things that you do not know about. I would like to tell you about them. I *need* to tell you about them. I hope you can understand what I am about to say. I hope that you can believe what I am about to say. That even though you may think I am indifferent at times, even though you may feel that the space between us is larger at some times than at others, I want you to know that here, in my heart, it is slowly closing. You may perceive me as not being in your presence, but in my heart I am there.

You are right; there is a reticence in me. There is a need for me to feel secure, a need for me to fully trust someone. There is also a desire in me to belong. But somehow I am not showing what I want to be like when I am with you. I hope you have some patience. I hope you can see that I am trying. I hope that I do not lose you.

Perhaps what I am about to say will make you give me some time. I hope that you believe me. I hope that you understand. It is about me. It is about my life. It is personal; something I have not shared with others.

Whenever it was, whenever it arrived, it just turned up. I could not see it. I could not understand it. I was not even aware of it. It just seems to have happened.

I remember that time, that time when I was young, when I was a child. It was then, it was around that time. We had moved. We kept moving from one place to another: everything seemed so strange, everything seemed so unfamiliar. There were people... new people... many of them... They were strangers... they were people, people I did not know... so many faces... changing so quickly... no time to get to know any one... Whom could I trust? No one.

New friends appeared. Then they were gone. Then I was

alone. It was as if they had died. As if I could be with people but as I was with them... they died. As I got to know them... they died.

A fear... A fear came into me. I do not know exactly when, I do not know exactly how, but I had this fear. I did not know at the time. I could not express myself... but now that I look back... I can see it lived in every cell of my body. If I spoke... if I was with others... they would disappear... As if they had died. It seemed like every time I became familiar with someone... they would be gone... disappear... no longer want to be near me.

I had a fear. It was there. I do not know why, but it felt as if I was trapped. By being *me*, others would disappear. By being *me*, it felt as if I were abandoned. No one could see. No one could understand. It seemed no one cared.

When we eventually stayed in one place, when people were around me, I could not speak. I would struggle, I would fight to say something, but all that happened was silence. All that happened inside was chaos.

There were times, as a child, when I was in school, that I could not talk. I could not talk to teachers. I could not talk to others. I could not talk for many years. I was silent. I was trapped. But all they saw was someone who *wanted* to be quiet, someone who *chose* to be silent, some one who was *being awkward*, and someone *doing it intentionally*. They thought I was shy but I was not. At home I was loud: I shouted, I screamed, I talked a lot. At home it was safe. At home it was familiar.

At school, the children... They were not nice. They did things, they used to say things. They said that I was 'dumb'. They said that I was 'stupid'. They said I was a... 'freak'. They teased me. They bullied me. They threw things at me. They laughed at me. I was not like them. I was silent.

Every time they insulted me, every time they threw something at me, I screamed, I shouted, I cried, I cried hard. All they heard was nothing. All they saw was an expressionless face. The anger did not show. The unhappiness did not show. The tears failed to appear. They continued... they continued.

I remember a time when I was playing with others. It was at school. We were playing. Although I could not speak, I joined in. I could point and gesture. I could be a part of others, be with them, belong. I was free inside. Free from anxiety. I was free and I just wanted to play, to 'be with' other children. It was nice. I was happy and I did not have to speak.

Then they looked at me. They saw a 'freak' playing with them. Then they did not want me. They did not want to 'catch' something. They teased me and laughed at me. They picked me up and took me to a rubbish bin. They put me inside and then... then they laughed. My tears did not show. My anger did not appear. My words did not manifest. All they saw was my face — expressionless. They did not see that a part of me had died. They did not see that they were destroying me inside.

I was only a child... and I hated myself. I was not a bad person. I just could not do things. I just wanted to be liked. But all that was there was an ever-widening space between myself and others.

It was not one incident or two, but many, every day — the laughs, the teasing, the ridicule. Every day something else would disintegrate inside me. Every day I tried desperately to communicate with others. Every day something held me back. How can I tell you what it was like? How can I express to you what it felt like?... Can you imagine that you are prepared to die rather than talk? That talking becomes more painful than death itself? Can you understand that? Can you?... I was so afraid. Yet... yet... at home I could speak.

I remember the times at school, the times when I needed to use the bathroom... I remember... so much pain... so much humiliation. How could I ask? How could I request? I had to raise my hand. I had to speak. I would rather die than speak. What was I to do? What could I do?

I had no control over the fear — I was paralysed with it, no expression on my face to tell others I needed help — trapped. I would sit in no man's land for a long time, until the bell rang. I would sit in no man's land until... until I was humiliated. I would sit there struggling... fighting... crying... wanting to die. It was easier to be humiliated than to speak. And when I was humiliated, I felt shame, I felt embarrassment. I felt all this and I had to return to the place of humiliation the next day... and the next. I was different... I could be laughed at.

Then there was that time when I was at home. I remember it because I was safe there, a place where I could talk, where I could shout and scream, where I had no fear — it was *my* place. It was that time when I overheard my parents talking. I remember that night. I overheard my parents talking about me, talking about their child. I heard them say some words... They were not nice. I heard those words, those nine words that have been forever branded on my mind. I heard those nine words that crushed the very core of me, the very core of my being. They destroyed the only place of safety I had. They were words, just words... simply words. How could words ever hurt? I heard them...'I do not think he will have a future'.

The only people, in the only place, that I felt safe with, nearly killed me with those nine words. What do you do? What do you do when your whole world of 'safe' people shatters in a space of nine words, when those you care for break the last bonds of trust and emotional attachment to the world you are in?... I was devastated... They could not even see my suffering — I was expressionless.

I remember going to a mirror. I looked at myself. I wanted to see what others saw — I wanted to see what I could not understand, to understand why people could not 'see' me, why they could not see who I was — that I was only a child... That I was also a human being. And when those nine words repeated themselves in my mind, I saw something in the mirror... I saw... I saw something that affected me profoundly: I saw some distance in my eyes. It was distance between who I saw in the mirror and my inner self.

I could not let anyone else see this. I could not let anyone else see that I was fractured, that I was lost. I did not trust anyone. How could I let them see this split in my very being? It was *my* split, it was *my* fracture and *no one* had the right to laugh at it, to laugh at the last part of my existence that I could hold on to. I was almost dead inside... Only this last vestige of contact with others.

I remember then... that I had to go to school. It was a struggle. It was a fight — almost to the death. There was no safe place, not even at home. I remember going into school, wanting to speak. It was emotional, speaking was emotional. And, as I spoke, I would 'reveal' myself to others. I recall... I recall saying something... it felt like I was screaming... like I was shouting. I nearly died in the process. And all any one heard was a whisper. All anyone heard was a mumble. All they could do was laugh. They laughed at my feeble voice. They laughed at me — at my pathetic-ness. Some were shocked. Some were shocked at my speech... shocked at my emotional speech... shocked at my emotions. My emotions, my feelings, seemed to cause some 'horror', some offence, to others. In that moment, in that instant, my trust of the world ended.

When the world around you is hurting you, when the world around you refuses to see who you are, how can you trust others? How can you trust people? When all you have is your family, when all you have is your family who cannot see who you are and they, they continue to hurt you, they hurt you... then... then trust becomes meaningless. And because of that meaninglessness I retreated into myself. It is safe there: no one to harm you, no one to let you down. It is a place I often go to. It is a place I often go to when I am with others. A place I go to when I want to forget others.

When I am there, when I am in that safe place, it is like reading a book. It is like reading a book that you are engrossed in: you can have a relationship with yourself, with that book, with someone or something that cannot hurt you... in exclusivity. It is like reading a book that you are captivated by — you lose the world around you, you even lose the awareness that you are reading. I used to get so absorbed in myself. And I used to do that not out of vanity, but as survival. That survival for me was about escaping the fetters of my existence, the fetters suffocating my being; the fetters that are my anxiety towards other people.

I have never felt like I belong to anyone. I have never felt like anyone has ever wanted me. I am so used to coming into and out from my self-absorption that being with others becomes difficult. I am so used to my self-absorption that when I am in the presence of others I often stop myself being with them because I seem to retreat.

It has become automatic now. It sometimes happens without my control. It happens without my awareness. I seem to do it now out of habit. I seem to do it now as if it was a part of my character. And maybe it is this — this withdrawal into myself — that you experience. But, *I am here* with you, trust me... believe me... I am here... I am present.

You see, I have missed a lifetime of socialising. I have missed a lifetime of being with others. There are certain skills that I may not possess. There are certain signals that I may not be able to perceive in others. It is as if those fetters still bind my existence. I feel as if I am suffocating, not just in the fear that I have but also in my inability to be with others.

I know I have been terrified by others, but in that fractured part of myself there is a desire to want to be with people. I want to be with others without the pain. I want to be with others without the hurt. For so long, I have been curled up in a corner, that lonely corner of my being. For so long, I have wanted someone to hold me. For so long, I have wanted someone to love me. I was a person. I *am* a person. I needed to feel human. I needed to be loved — even a smile, a smile would have meant so much.

I know that I am older now. I know that I can communicate better. I now know how I should behave — but knowing how to be with others and actually being with others are so far apart.

I am here. I am here because I want to be. I am here because when I first met you, I saw something that wanted me to come out of that corner. I saw something that was sincere and genuine. I saw something that I had to take a major risk for. I saw an expression on your face... I saw an expression on your face that reached into my heart... An expression that touched me, an expression that felt as if your arms were around me... I saw your smile.

I am not sure how you will react to what I have said. I am not sure if you want to run away, run away from me — run away from... a 'freak'.

Whilst I am here with you as an adult, there is still a little child inside, trying to move away from that corner. Whilst I am present here with you, there is a little boy tugging at me, trying to pull me back, not because of you but because he hasn't learnt to trust, because he is full of fear.

Thank you for sharing this with me. Thank you for talking to me about it. You are most certainly not a 'freak'. You have no need to be worried. You have a lot to be admired for. You have gone through a lot in your life and yet you have not turned it into anger or aggression. You have had so much difficulty in life and yet have remained so gentle.

I can only picture and understand this fear that you have had. I will try to be here for you. I will try to show you as we are together that there is some comfort in being with others. And for that child in the corner, I shall encourage him to come forward — to enter this space that is between us. For this adult in front of me, I shall be patient. And hopefully... hopefully, you may learn to trust me. Perhaps... perhaps, as you look in the mirror from now on, you will see the distance in your eyes shortening.

III

Empty Space

You once said to me that you wanted to be with someone. To be with someone so that you could avoid loneliness, so that you could feel valued, so that you could feel like a woman. In the times when we have seen each other, the times when we have met, you seem not to want to talk about 'being' with each other. I am here and yet you seem apart from me.

It feels like every time I want to talk about being with each other, about being close to one another, about the intimacy of a relationship, it seems as if you want to avoid the subject. I do not know how you feel about it. You may not want to tell me. You may not be able to tell me. It is as if you cannot trust me.

You mentioned your sister to me once. Perhaps it is difficult for you to let go of her. Perhaps she means too much to you to allow me into your heart. Yet... yet you say to me that you cannot exist without others. But I am here. Here for you. I am the 'other'. The 'other' who is attracted to you.

It seems to me that though I am here for you, you still remain lonely; lonely in a way I do not understand. Maybe I do not make you feel like a woman. Maybe I am not what you expected. Maybe you do not value me.

I am not sure if you can trust me. I am not sure if you can talk to me. I am not sure why, when I am with you, you are still lonely.

I feel I can trust you. I feel I can talk to you. You have done what others have not. You have been open with me. You have been honest with me. You have told me something about yourself that is very private to you. You have let me in. Let me in without knowing too much about me.

You took the risk of allowing me to listen. You took the risk of letting me know about a vulnerability you have. In that action alone, I know that you are strong. Strong enough to say some very important things to me. Strong enough to listen to me.

I want to share something about me. I would like you to listen. I hope that you understand.

You asked me why I feel lonely at times, why I feel lonely when you are there. It is difficult for me to say. It may be difficult for you to understand. It may be difficult for you to understand that I can be with others and with you, that I like being with others and with you, and yet I can be apart from them — that I can be apart from you.

Inside... here... in my heart... I am lonely. Not the loneliness that one has when one is not around others, but a loneliness that is a part of my existence. A loneliness that exists regardless of where you are and who you are with.

It is a loneliness in which you want to reach out, a loneliness that cannot reach far enough. It is a loneliness in which there is a sheet of glass between you and the world around you.

You are there — laughing, smiling, crying. But in an instant, in a moment, you realise the very coldness of your existence: you are there and you are not there, both at the same time; you are participating and yet observing from without; with others and yet not being with them. Just like I am with my sister: she is here and, yet, not here.

As I wake up and look beside me, I get that feeling — in that instant, in that moment. As I become conscious I become aware of my loneliness. When I am awake, I am lonely. In that moment, I know I am in the world that is in front of me and yet I feel I am observing myself participating in that world. I see this happening from a distance.

At times, when I am with somebody, I ask myself 'have I been here with that person?'– that person who is lying beside me – but at all times I ask myself, 'why am I lonely here with that person?'

It is that sheet of glass that is always there... that sheet of glass between me and that person... that person who is lying beside me. In that instant, in that moment, the person who is lying beside me becomes meaningless.

27

You asked me why I do not want to be intimate with you − I do. But I am afraid. I am afraid that you will become one of those meaningless people. I do not want that. I do not want you to be there so that you can fill my loneliness. I want you to be there so that I can be with you, so that I can feel that you are with me.

This loneliness, that prevents me from being with you, is like a fractured part of me. That part of me that cannot be healed. That fractured part of me that is me. As I am me, I am lonely. Inescapable.

Some days I imagine, I imagine that this is not so; I imagine that I can break down that sheet of glass. I imagine that I can find somebody, someone like you. Somebody who I can be with. That somehow, because of one person, it will all disappear; that I can be rescued.

What I would do so that I can feel connected with somebody! To be with them. For them to be a part of me. To be in a genuine, authentic... true relationship.

I have not told you this, yet. I do not know how you will feel. But I believe you are strong. I believe I can trust you. Trust you more than anyone else that I have known.

It happened a while ago... It happened a long time ago... I had a sister... she was my twin... I killed her.

She was young... so young... I did not give her a chance to live... She was helpless... she had no choice... I did not give her a choice.

They told me... They told me that... the cord that bound us together... the cord that provided us with life... with life inside our mother... They told me that I had the larger cord... That due to some complication... I had the better blood supply... That I had the better chance... A better chance to live.

She died because of me.

She died. I could feel her dying. I could feel her dying slowly. I was there... I was there...

I was taking her blood... Taking her life from her. It was as if I was draining her, draining her of her life... Draining her slowly. It was like waiting for death to happen. It was like wanting death to happen, as if I wanted it to happen, for me to be the cause of her death. It is as if I killed her. As if I killed her slowly...

She could not survive. How could she survive? I took her blood from her, I took her life. I took it slowly. She remained quiet. She said nothing...

...

I knew the moment she died. I knew it. I could feel it. I could sense it — that moment when her heart stopped beating. I took the last part of her life. She had no choice.

She had said nothing up until that point, the point at which I took the last part of her life. However, in that instant, in that moment... I 'heard' her. She cried.

She tried to say something to me — too late...

I heard her. I hear her. At times when I get lonely... I hear her... I hear her — she reminds me... She reminds me that I took the last drops of blood from her... Reminding me that I took the last essence of life from her.

She died.

She died and I could not reach out to hold her... She died when I could not speak... She died when I could not say 'goodbye'. She just died.

It is strange... just as I 'heard' her... I knew I was alone... alone without her, without my sister. She was there... dead... Some part of me missing... gone... ceasing to exist. It happened in that moment... That first moment I opened my eyes and could not sense that she was there lying beside me... some part of me ceased to exist... gone... Lost...

Then... Then... I had to wait... wait with loneliness... Wait alone...

I could not escape... escape the loneliness... just me... loneliness... Loneliness — a part of me.

I wanted to leave... Wanted to leave that loneliness... Wanted to leave that deathbed. I wanted to escape, to flee... To flee that loneliness... that deathbed... To flee from her... from the one I took life from... To flee from the one I loved.

I wanted to escape... I <u>needed</u> to escape... But I was trapped... trapped with a dead body... Trapped with a corpse.

...

When I was being born, I felt trapped again. I was trapped – trapped in the birth canal. Could not move, could not escape.

I wanted to be the first to be born... It was not nice in there... It was not nice in there sharing it with the dead... I wanted to leave it behind.

Leaving was not easy. It was too much. It was difficult. Struggling... fighting to get out. Everything was closing in on me... surrounding me... suffocating me... suffocating me slowly... no room for me.

Up to that point, I had known life as loneliness... life as living with the dead; but I needed to know life – without loneliness... Without the dead.

I needed air to bring life... I was leaving death but I wanted life... life to breathe... to escape the loneliness... To escape the one I loved... The one I took life from.

I was unable to gasp air... I could not open my mouth... I wanted to open my mouth. But I was stuck... stuck in the birth canal... stuck in between life and death... it seemed like an eternity... I was alone.

Eventually, when my head was free, I was unable to gasp... gasp the air that I needed... Unable to get the life that I wanted... There was something stopping me... stopping me from being born... something pressing on my throat... something compressing my windpipe... something stopping me from breathing... stopping me from gaining life...

It was my mother... she was choking me... it was as if she did not want me to be born... My head was free but my body was not... preventing me from being born... prevented by the thing that was pressing on my throat... I was between life and death... Struggling.

I could not breathe... I could not breathe the air that I wanted... I could not breathe the air that I needed... My mother – she was choking me... it was as if she wanted to kill me... as I had killed my sister.

But when I was born – I cried... I cried in relief... I cried because... because in that instant, that moment... that moment that I was born... I became cold... It was very cold... Life was cold. I cried when I realised life was cold. As I cried, I could feel her – my sister... I could feel her tug at me... tug on the cord that bound us together. It reminded me... it reminded me in my cry... when I was cold... that some part of me was missing... In that moment, life was cold and lonely.

Now – I cannot be with anyone. When I am... When I hold someone, it is as if they are dead... As if there is no one there... just an empty space... It means nothing. It feels like nothing... It feels lonely when I am with someone.

Because of her... Because of my twin... the twin whom I had shared an intimate space with... Because of her — I had to share that intimate space with the dead.

When I have been with someone... When I have been intimate with someone... It is as if I have been intimate with an empty space... a meaningless relationship... As if I have been intimate with death. It is as if death — what I had left behind, all those years ago — it is as if death wants to enter me... to enter my birth chamber.

I do not want it to be like that with you... I do not want this to happen with you. I want to be with you. I want to be intimate with you, but I am afraid. I am afraid at times, afraid that it might be meaningless, afraid of a meaningless intimacy. But I do not want to lose you.

You will not lose me... You will not lose me.

I hear what you have said. I cannot take away the feelings that you have, nor would I want to. They are your feelings. They are your life. They are you. And it is you I want to be with.

I cannot replace your twin. I cannot replace your sister, nor can I bring to you that part of you that you feel is missing.

Even though I am trying to understand the pain you are suffering, I am not sure if I would be able to fully understand the loss of a sister or brother before birth.

I just hope that you understand that... whatever you cannot resolve... I want to be with you... that I want to be there for you. I want you to know that the empty space you feel, that space in which you want to hold someone who is no longer there — I want you to know that I want to fill that space for you. That whenever you find the need to hold that space, you can come to me. It is no longer a space for you to be alone, but a space for us.

I want to hold you. Can I hold you?

...

This is how I would like us to be... In each other's arms. I do not pretend to be your sister. I do not pretend to be your twin but someone who is on your side, someone who is on your side of that sheet of glass.

Thank you.

We will be together. We will be intimate. It will take some time, but we will be together. Perhaps soon.

IV

Afraid to Speak

We have been together for some time. We have known each other for a while. I know you have begun to trust me more. I know that I am beginning to trust you.

I can see how at times you may have had difficulties in saying things. I have seen you in situations where you take part in social intercourse, talking with some verve and vitality. I have seen you be enthusiastic and loud in some circumstances. I have also at times seen you struggle in an environment. I have seen you in those environments struggle to express yourself. I have seen you struggle to express yourself with me.

I wish, though, that the world could see what I can see. I wish you could show the world that side of you – that side of you that seems to be free.

I know that there is some part of you that wants to hide itself; that you seem to want to hide yourself away from the world. But I also know that there are some parts of you that you are hiding from me. You may not do it intentionally, but that is how it seems to me. It is as if you do not trust me. It is as if the time I have known you has meant nothing to you. Perhaps I mean nothing to you.

I know you can express yourself in your needs to me. I know they are important. I also know that there are some words I need to hear. That after such a time I long to hear them and I have to hear them... hear them from you.

I know that the words I want you to say, you do feel. But sometimes knowing that is not enough – not enough to fill my void, to fill my heart, to fill the gap between you and me.

Those words that I need to hear, they are not 'present' here with me. I need them to be. I would like you to say those words. They would mean so much, knowing they are for me.

I am too afraid to say those words. It is as if I cannot say those words, as if I do not want to say those words.

Once I say the words I feel, they are there, in the open, hovering in this space before us, forever in time. And once they have reached you, they become permanent sentiments of my being.

They are no longer just my reality. They become yours, too, and anyone else who hears them.

For me to say them would be like me revealing something personal. To reveal something of my emotions — those that have been shut away for a long time, those that have been locked away. They would no longer belong to me. They would no longer be mine. They would no longer have their meaning, slowly decaying over a period of time, vanishing into some kind of oblivion.

I am not sure if I can risk it. Not sure if I want to open a window to my inner self. It would be too much to bear; to know that some part of me risks insignificance.

If I were to speak those words that I feel, they would linger in this space, still attached to me, to myself, lingering until... until they are received. They would be there for you to take, for you to capture. To take something that belongs to me. To take something that is mine. To take something that will never leave me, something that is connected to me, that has been mine... and mine alone.

To capture them would be like hijacking them, to have them out of my control, to take them without my will. It would then be like you pulling them away from me... tugging forcefully to elicit some emotion. Disturbing something that is so very much a part of my being. It would be like placing a finger in waters that have been still for thousands of millennia, causing ripples to disturb sediments that have settled.

I get confused. I *am* confused. I need those sediments to be settled. Yet, I am touched by feelings I thought I would never have, feelings that do not feel safe. Not that they are bad, just that they cause ripples. Ripples in an otherwise settled pain.

I have feelings for you. I do not know how to communicate them.

I know that those words in this space will cause me pain. I know that the moment I think about speaking them will be the moment I shall experience the pain. I am caught between the desire to say and the desire not to say. That is the hardest battle... To risk everything and to be available to judgement or to feel safe with something that I know. Am I to lose you or am I to lose me?

By speaking them and having them received, it would mean that someone wants to tug at me, to tug at my emotions. It would feel abusive. Perhaps truth is abusive.

I want to speak the truth. I want to say those words to you.

I am afraid that when I... I... when I 'exposé myself to you... that I will be laughed at... be refused... not be accepted. That you will, in some rage of anger, at some other time, throw it back in my face... belittle the way I feel.

I am afraid that you will ignore my feelings... ignore me. That would be the worst — to have taken so much effort and to risk a lot — to have expressed what I have wanted and longed to do... and then to be ignored.

I am also afraid that you may not believe me. That something so meaningful for me — my love for you — would just not be believed.

It would be to risk everything and be humiliated, to be judged and be embarrassed.

I have that fear. I have the fear that the words that linger between us, once I have spoken them, arrive in you with either disbelief or are ignored, or that at some point in time they will have less of an impact or become meaningless to you.

I have the fear that my pain and the abusiveness are insignificant. That I am insignificant.

I have not been able to express those words because of the way I feel, because of the pain. My sincerity gives me this fear. My sincerity is about the pain I will suffer when I say those words to you. My sincerity is my fear.

I can say those words — 'I love you'. But I say them without my feelings, just like I would say 'there's a tree' or 'here's a flower'. You may not receive these words any differently, but for me they are mere words. And when these 'mere' words linger in this space between us in the same way, you may have no way of knowing how they have been expressed. But when I do say them, I would not utter them if they did not feel genuine enough.

I want those words to roam around us... entwining us... To be heard by you and for you to appreciate the significance of them... For them to become a bridge from my heart to yours.

At the very core of my being I feel lonely, just as you do. I feel isolated in this world of ours. I feel alienated by life itself. I feel I have no right but the coldness of my existence, and neither you nor anyone else can hurt me behind my self-protection.

When I am with you, you stir up the pain. It becomes tumultuous and unfamiliar to deal with. It is not like the other pain. It is a kind pain. A kind pain that is uneasy inside me. It is something beautiful. It is something that I have never felt before.

It is painful because it is the first time I have felt it. It is as if I have been touched for the first time. It is as if I have been validated as being human: that I am a human being... that I can be touched.

You made me somewhat significant. You have made me 'someone'.

But there is always a 'but'. My years of fear and pain will not allow me to say those words with strong sentiment. Though time may be my healer, it is also my wound.

I do not want to be exposed to further pain. To risk opening that wound. To risk opening that wound would be to risk my pain, the pain that I feel comfortable with.

I shall whisper those words to you. I shall whisper them so that they can escape from me, so that I can allow them to escape, so that my breath can carry them into this space between us.

When I whisper them, you must hear them.

For you not to hear them, and for you to ask me to repeat them, would only serve to crush me, for you to pull on my words, to coax them, without my will. It would make me feel that my words do not mean enough to you, make me feel that they are not significant, that I am not significant: I would have to close my eyes with tears.

These words... these words... these words that I have... are for you... 'I love you'.

Thank you. I love you, too.

I love everything about you.

I love you. I love your pain. I love your suffering. I love your heart and I love your mind. I love your body and I love your soul. I love those eyes of yours. I love that mouth. I love your muscular body. I love you.

Those words you say, that I hear... I welcome them. I do not pretend to pull on them. I am as equally touched by your words as you are by mine.

Those words that have lingered in the space between us have, for me, only closed that gap.

I know it must have been difficult for you... to say what you felt. I do not suppose that I know what it means to you to say those words that you said, but I do know that I will forever love you. Whereas time has wounded you, you are healing me.

I hope that you can understand what I am saying. I hope that you can understand what I am feeling. I hope you can understand that I have no intention of making any demands on you... to pull or force you into feeling something.

You are my love. You are my life.

Don't, please don't.

I hear what you are saying. I like what you are saying. But it feels too much to deal with... too much to handle all at once. It feels like I am being suffocated.

I have said the words I speak feel like they are tugging at my pain, but so are the words that I hear. So are the words that travel from your heart to mine. When they leave your heart they are clear. When they arrive in mine they disrupt the still waters, making them unclear. I feel touched. I feel I have been given something so precious. Something that is just for me. It makes me want to sit here and cry. Even though others have said they loved me, it is only with you that I have felt its true meaning.

V

Touched in Intimacy

I know you have expressed the desire to want to be intimate. And I have heard the words that you have said. There is something inside me that wants me to be with you also. There is something inside me that wants the intimacy that you will bring.

I want to be with someone whom I can live with. I want to be with someone whom I can live passionately with, to be able to feel them in every cell of my body, to be breathing with them with every breath I take. I want to be with someone whose heart will beat as one with mine, who, when I close my eyes, will always be there in my mind. Who, when I shed tears, will always be there to wipe them away. Who, when I laugh, will laugh too. I want to be with somebody not for the immediacy but for the whole duration of time.

There are moments in life that seem so precious. There are moments which seem so infrequent. It is in those precious moments when you can find someone like that. It is those precious moments that must last a lifetime. Those moments only last that duration when someone respects you, when someone can be trusted – trusted with the honesty of the way you feel. You are my precious moment and I need you to last a lifetime.

I know that you are gentle. I know that you are considerate. I know that you have been honest with me. But trust – trust comes with time. Although I have learnt to trust you, there is something I would like you to hear. Something that I hope you will understand. Something I need you to understand. Understand so that we can be as 'one'. To also be as one in that private space that we want to share; the space in which intimacy can take place.

I know that in the past, trust has perhaps become meaningless to you, that you may have had difficulty in trusting people around you. I know that you have taken some brave steps with me, that you have taken risks that have lead you to come out of your comfort zone, to come out of it to express some very private things to me. It is in this alone that I know how much you want to be with me. It is in this alone that I can see that you are moving away from that corner, breaking away from your fears, those fetters of your existence.

It is from knowing that that I know you can understand. I know you can understand that I, as a woman, also need to feel some semblance of trust: a trust that will allow us to share that same space; a trust for us to be as one in our intimacy.

I do trust you. I trust you but I am saying this because I know you are kind and gentle. I know you will always be considerate. I am saying this because I want to, because I need to, because, with you, I want to ensure that you are not an empty space. That when I wake up, when I open my eyes, I will see that you are lying next to me on this side, __my__ side, of the glass. That there will also be some warmth brought to my existence.

When you close your eyes, when they are shut, the world disappears from your mind. Imagine... Imagine what it would be like if your eyes remained closed for a very long time. Would you remember the world? Would you have a memory of it? Would it have faded? As the world disappears from our minds, so has the memory of being touched disappeared for me. The memory seems to have faded. It seems to have vanished into some kind of oblivion.

I have been touched before. I have had hands upon my body. But this was something which was just physical – like something you do when you pick up things. There has been an absence of any meaning, of any warmth; something that lifts me out of my loneliness, something that makes me feel secure, something that would make me feel like a woman: feel loved and not abandoned.

I have been in intimacy. I have been touched in intimacy. But when I have been with others, they have not meant as much as you have to me. They are people who I have been with. They are people who have just wanted me for something. They are people who have not wanted me for me.

It is when I am with them that it has felt like I have not been with them. It has felt like I have not been in union with them, that I have not been in congress with them. That being intimate with them was somehow without feeling, without passion – without meaning. It was an act that I had to go through, something that my body needed, something that I wanted. But my mind was never satisfied; there was no pleasure, there was no joy, my emotions remained dissatisfied. It is something that has left me with emptiness.

I have not felt that I have been touched for a long time. That intimacy has become just that — simply an act devoid of sensual pleasure. Touch did not mean anything to them; wanting me for other things did.

I want it to be real with you. I want our intimacy to be about pleasure, about your needs as well as mine. I want it to be about meaning and about respect.

Sometimes I have felt as if I am not human; that my basic human need cannot even be fulfilled. That there has not been any respect for me in my life to make me feel loved. That by not feeling loved, by not feeling touched, I have become untouchable and those whom I have been in close proximity with have been the source of my anguish; they have been the source of my longing, of my pain, of my need to be touched.

I do not know if it was ever about love. I do not know if their hands ever expressed their love for me. Perhaps it was for the fulfilment they could achieve. Either way, somewhere, sometime, it gets so confusing to know when; touch somehow lost its meaning for me. What is my body without its need? Who am I without the contact of others? I was lost.

It is not their fault. Perhaps I had not been ready to feel touched. Perhaps I cannot acknowledge the meaning of their touch. Maybe I will never be able to.

It is not just about the physical; it is about the emotional. It is about how I have valued myself — how I have sought those who perpetuate my insatiate need. There is something inside me; something that seems not to appreciate the touch of others. Perhaps I do not want to be associated with the happiness of others, and by not wanting that I deny myself the belief it is happy to be touched.

But there are other reasons that prevent me from feeling content with someone's touch. Perhaps it was when I was sharing that space with my sister. Perhaps it was that.

Yes, I remember. I remember it. It was when she was dying, when I was slowly killing her. I think she reached out. I think she reached out to tell me to stop. She was trying to touch me; she was trying to make me aware that she needed me.

I remember. I remember that she was trying to touch me. I remember she was dying. I remember her touch. It was as if death was touching me. Because of that touch, I felt so cold and lonely. It was cold and lonely inside there. Yet... yet... When I left the birth chamber, when I left the birth canal, the moment I left her behind, the moment I entered this world, I could feel the coldness of life on my skin.

Now, when people touch me, I do not want to be reminded of it. I do not want to be reminded that through touch there can only be cold and loneliness, that through touch there can only be death.

I know deep down that this is not true, but it is how I feel. That because of the intimacy of that shared space, whenever I experience a similar intimacy, I shall be frightened of someone's touch.

As I became a woman, as I grew into an adult, I knew that there were other needs that needed fulfilling. That I had to experience those needs so that I could feel like a woman, so that I could identify with womanhood. It was in those needs that it became painful.

How do I be intimate and yet avoid touch? How do I avoid the sort of touch someone wants to give because of their need, their need to be 'loved', their need for intimacy, their need for closeness? In reaching out for their needs, they would want to touch me, and for me it would be about coldness and loneliness – it would be about death.

How could I have dealt with that? How could I have dealt with the pain of wanting womanhood and not wanting to be touched? Is there comfort in being touched by death?... Touch... touch... touch has become meaningless. It had to be meaningless, meaningless; because of the pain of death.

I don't know if I have ever been satisfied in intimacy. Sometimes I do not care, but I know now, with you, I am experiencing something inside that I am not used to. I am experiencing something that makes me want to be with you, something that feels like some gentle flutters. Something that makes me want to smile every time I see you. Touching, now, seems to be about my needs, my desires, my wants, and I know I want you.

Sometimes I think that if I touch you, perhaps I shall be spreading the cold and loneliness. That if I touch you, perhaps I shall be spreading death to your experience of intimacy. I do not want that. I want to 'be with' you and I want it to be meaningful. That is why I am waiting. I wait for these good feelings inside me to dominate.

I want my anxiety of touch to subside; I want to see you when we are in union and not my sister.

Sometimes I imagine being with you. Sometimes I imagine being touched by you. Sometimes I imagine there is happiness there: that there is happiness in touching. That by touching we can close this space that is between us. That hopefully there will no longer be me and you but 'us'. That our skins, our bodies, our selves no longer have to be lonely, no longer have to go hungry.

I would like that... I would like that very much.

Thank you. Thank you for telling me about your concerns. They are indeed very private to you, and I can see why you felt you had to share them with me.

I hope that you can learn to trust me fully, to trust me to the point where those good feelings will dominate. You do not have to force yourself to tell me; you do not have to jump at the first opportunity when you feel that you can trust me. It only becomes meaningful to me when I know you feel safe enough to tell me, when you know inside the quality of my sincerity.

We have held hands before. We have held hands together. We have held them as we have walked, as we have sat, as we have cuddled. In those times that our hands have met all I have felt is your warmth, your tenderness of touch, the softness of your skin.

For me, that has been the most beautiful thing about this space that we have been trying to close. It is here that I know you have begun to trust me. It is here that I have begun to trust you.

It has been difficult for me to trust another. It has been difficult for me to believe in others. They have always hurt me, they have always disappeared; it seems that they always destroy some part of me. But in holding your hands, in being with you, some meaningfulness in trust has come back; some desire to trust has come back. I hope you can see that.

Yes, yes, I have seen your face become more expressive. I have seen the way you look at me. It is a nice way. It is a caring way.

Whenever you feel that those good feelings inside will dominate, whenever you feel that my hands can express both my needs and yours, I would like you to tell me. Just as my face has begun to show you that I can trust you, so I would like your hands to tell me. Perhaps through some gentle caress of my palms as we hold hands. I would like your hands to tell me when you would like to wake up and see me lying next to you.

It is so nice, the way you take away the anxiety from me. It is so nice that you have asked me to make a simple gesture to let you know when we can close this space between us. It is so nice that I do not have to get anxious about expressing some words, to even think about how to express them. It is nice that through a simple touch, things will be okay.

I know that words have been difficult for you in the past. But I would like to express some now. They are words we will use. Words that will take away some of the difficulty you may have in expressing them. These are words that we will try to use instead of 'I love you'. Just as you have asked me to make a simple gesture, this will be our simple gesture to one another. These will be our words. Words that will be private to us, that, when we express them, will touch my heart and your heart. These words that I have, they are for you. They come from my heart... One four three.

VI

Talking in Her Ear

Do you know what I would like? Do you know what I would like to do?

Tell me. Tell me what you would like to do.

I would like you to close your eyes. I would like you to close them for me. Close your eyes — close your eyes... Close them. I am just going to walk behind you, walk behind you and say something in your ear. Close your eyes... Listen...

I want to take you into the bedroom...

... To stand you up against the wall. I want to raise your hands up above your head, holding them together — as if they were tied.

For you to shut your eyes — as if you were...blindfolded.

I would move your legs... away from the wall.

Then I would part them — your hands still 'tied' above your head.

I would close my eyes... and want to kiss you... gently... on your forehead: at the top... in the centre... to the left... then to the right.

To kiss you between your eyes.

I want to kiss you on your closed eyelids — the left, then the right.

To kiss you below your eyes... and to the side of them.

I want to kiss you on your cheeks, first one and then the other.

To kiss the tip of your nose.

I want to hold your face... with both my hands... and kiss you... on your lips.

Yes! The kiss.

I want you to part your lips when you kiss me... so that I can hold your top lip in between my lips... so that I can run my tongue along the edge of your top lip... And then... slowly... run my tongue along... the underside of your lip. Stopping at the centre... moving it up as far as it will go... lifting your lip outwards... and back down again... tickling — stimulating those sensitive nerves.

I would still want to hold your top lip in between my lips... pulling it forward carefully, stretching and holding it... my tongue caressing your lip... gently... moving across its length... teasing your lip... inside my mouth... and then... letting go.

To kiss you on your lips again. Then on your cheek... your jaw... behind your jaw — on your neck — under your ears...

To take your ear lobe... into my mouth.

To kiss you on your neck... behind your lobes, and to slowly spell the word 'L-O-V-E'... with my tongue, just there... behind your ear. Then to gently blow... on the traces of the wet saliva.

I would open my eyes and want to turn you around... so that you face the wall. Your hands still tied... and legs... still apart.

I want to untie your hands and bring them back down behind you, behind me, bringing them together, as if your hands were tied yet again, trapping me in your arms, pressing myself against you.

I want to pull back your hair... and kiss you behind your ears... to press my lips, softly, on your neck... to delicately suck on your skin... just enough to lift it away from you.

I want to kiss you just behind your ears... on your neck... on the side of your neck, working my way down to the bottom of your neck. Gently... slowly... giving you those little suction kisses... as I focus on your neck... for a short while... giving it some attention.

To move my fingers... fleetingly... from your shoulders... to your hands... as I kiss you from shoulder to shoulder. To caress... touch... stimulate the area... just above your elbows. To caress you... behind your wrists... softly circling the area... and then... to spell out the word 'S-E-X' with my finger.

To brush my fingers... along your fingers. To then stroke your little finger... from the outside of it... to its tip... and down the other side. Working my way from one finger... to the next.

I would slip my fingers in between yours. Free you from your 'shackles'... and tie your hands back above your head holding them there with one of my hands.

I want to kiss you... on your neck... down along your spine, between your shoulder blades... lower... and lower... until I arrive at your dress. Then... I will unzip you... and watch the rest of your back appear from behind the dress... blowing softly on your back as it reveals itself.

I want to place my hands inside your dress... at the base of your back. To move my hands around your sides... and then to feel your stomach... whilst I take your ear into my mouth. I want to play with your navel. To touch it with my forefinger... to move it, slowly, from the bottom, all the way around... and then back again.

To slide my hand... down to your underwear, lifting it... sliding down further... to touch your hair... to feel its softness. To move my hand down further, cupping, enveloping your sex... adjusting my posture... to give me better access. I would move my hand back upwards, using my middle finger to part your sex... moving it... allowing my finger tip to brush against your... *erect* clitoris.

Slide my hand back down... more firmly... parting it and then retreating. And in retreating... allow my finger to... somewhat insert itself... as I glide back up, seeking your clitoris to toy with.

I would guide my middle finger away from the top of your sex, around it... on the outside. Firstly, downwards... on the left... towards its base – leaving a trail of wetness behind. As it reaches its base, I would slither back upwards... this time on your right side... moving my finger to the top of your sex.

With my thumb and forefinger... clasp the left lip, near your clitoris... squeezing it gently, pressing it firmly... and then...

releasing it. Moving slightly further down... squeezing and releasing your lip... at various points... working my way down towards the base.

I would squeeze and release your right lip... starting from the base... pressing, freeing... as I move upwards towards your clit.

I would part your sex again... part it with my middle and index fingers... letting my palm press against your clitoris... as I insert my fingers into your womanhood, shifting your pelvis forward... to give me access.

As my fingers work their way inside... my thumb would rock itself gently against your clitoris. And when my fingers... find that 'bumpy'... 'corrugated'... ridge-like place, you know... that place, the one on the upper wall of your inner sex... I would let them rock in unison with my thumb... until your breath becomes shallow.

I would want to untie your left hand... moving it down... behind me... placing it on my...derrière... leaving my other hand tied to yours. Kissing you on your neck.

To slide my hands... up along your fingers... to the back of your hand... past your wrists... along your forearms... sliding up past your elbows... along your upper arm, making fleeting circles with my finger... on the sides of your shoulders.

To pull your dress strap off... off your shoulders, allowing it to slide down your arm. To kiss your shoulders... and then your arms... as I follow the strap down.

Then to lift your arm back up, so that it is tied to the other hand.

I want to untie your right hand... moving it down... behind me. Kissing you.

To slide my hands... up along your fingers... to the back of your hand... past your wrists... along your forearms... sliding up past your elbows... along your upper arm.

And with my teeth I would pull your dress strap off... sliding it down your arm... past your hand... then opening my mouth... allowing your dress to fall... to your ankles.

I would lift your feet so that I can move your dress away... from underneath you. Then kiss your ankle... circling it with the tip of my tongue... enclosing it with my lips. Kiss your ankle... kiss the area between your ankle and your heel.

I would then slide my hands from your ankles... touching you... feeling you... sliding my hands along the side of your calves... behind your knees... along the back of your thighs... towards your... your arse.

I want to feel your body... as I slide my hands under the seams of your underwear... from your backside... up towards your hip... over your hips... down towards the top of your front thigh... running my fingers down along the seams towards your... inner thigh... freeing your underwear... as I continue to caress your inner thigh, moving downwards.

To squeeze your thighs gently... moving my hands down to your knees... To move my hands back behind your knees... Stroking you up the back of your thighs, up towards your backside... placing my hands inside your underwear... touching your soft skin... lifting your underwear... away from your body... lifting it outwards at your hips... pulling down your underwear... exposing your sex... smelling its scent.

I want to stand up and hold your tied hands with one of my hands. With my other hand... to move my forefinger... slowly, tenderly... from between your cheeks... of your buttocks... caressing... fondling... your lower back... moving, gliding up along your spine... towards your bra... to un-strap it when I arrive... freeing your breasts.

I would like to turn you around. To then walk my fingers... from your navel... towards your breasts. As I arrive there... to lift your bra... away from your body... lifting it above your head, above your hands... freeing your hands momentarily, so that the bra can escape... leaving you naked.

As your bra is freed... I'll take your 'untied' hands and move them out and down behind you... holding them there... holding you in an embrace.

I would like to kiss you... on your forehead... to kiss you...

leaving a trail of kisses... from your temples... down the side of your face... in front of your ear... towards the corner of your jaw... down the side of your neck... back inwards, along your collar bone, to the bottom of your throat... kissing... gently, softly... moving downwards... to your... cleavage.

As I arrive in the middle of your cleavage... I would spell out '1 4 3' vertically, with the tip of my tongue... I would kiss you on your right breast... take it... into my mouth... squeezing your breast... with my tongue and the roof of my mouth... sucking... wetting your breast with my saliva...

I would kiss you... around your nipple... tracing the letter 'O' around your nipple... leaving it wet... so that you can feel the coldness of the air... as I gently breathe upon you.

I would want to take your breast, around your nipple... with my lips. To tease your nipple... to excite it... stimulating it... with my tongue.

To take your nipple between my teeth... to lift it... away from your breast... holding it gently... with my teeth... tugging at your breast. And then... to open my mouth... freeing your nipple, so that it can spring back... to your body.

I would then... want to move to your other breast... kissing you... on the inner side... of your right breast. And as my kisses move inwards... to try and catch... the flutter of my eyelashes... on your right nipple... teasing... stimulating... your nipple.

Kissing you... in between your breasts... to the inner side of your left breast... to the other breast... To do what I did to your left breast... as I did to your right...

I want to kiss you again... in the middle of your cleavage... slowly, softly... working my way down... down to the centre of your stomach... down towards your navel... circulating it... with my tongue... playing... poking my tongue... into your navel.

To kiss you... those gentle, soft, suction kisses... from your navel... slowly downwards... down to your waist... downwards... to your... your...

...My? My?

Open your eyes... Open them... Come with me... Take my hand...

VII

Every Second

Do you remember when you asked me to be with you, when you asked me to be intimate with you? You asked me this so that when we closed our eyes together we would reduce the space that was between us. It was then, in that moment, in that instant, when we were in union, that this space no longer existed. But we did not have to close our eyes for this to happen. The space was closing rapidly. It was closing rapidly since before that day when you first whispered into my ear, that day when we were drawn together.

Now, I am lying here with you. I am lying here in this other space — this space which is under your arms — this space where I now belong. This is the place that cements our togetherness: a space, yes, but our space, where we both are, where we are as one, where we both belong. It is here, when I am in our space, when I am in your arms, that I know the sheet of glass between myself and others is no more. It is as if it has melted away. It is as if it has vanished; as if it never existed.

It is important for me to know that, for you, the sheet of glass has vanished – that it has disappeared. That you can somehow think of our relationship in a way that you feel that sheet of glass has never existed. It is also important for me to know that in the time when we are together, when we are with one another, when I look into your eyes I see a glimpse, a fleeting glimpse, of some part of you. It is in that moment, in that instant, when our eyes are locked together, that I see the beauty of your heart. It is then that I see a snapshot of your soul. It is in that moment when we are 'with' one another, when we are in union, that a piece of my soul leaves me and enters you. It is in our congress when our souls meet.

It would seem that it is not just our souls that meet, but also our hearts. It would also seem, as we are locked in that moment, that as my heart beats so does yours; that as I breathe, so do you.

It is not just in the moment of our union that I feel that my breath and your breath are together. It is not just in the moment of our union that I feel that our hearts are as one. It has been in those moments and every other moment that I feel our love for one another has entwined and become one. It is where our souls are happy together. The togetherness has become a one-ness, and I hope that this one-ness will last forever. Time will carry my love for you.

Because of this feeling that I have, because of this time I refer to and because of my love for you, I have bought you something, something I hope will please you. This watch that I have here, it is for you. It is for you on this third anniversary of when we first met. It is about

the passing of time – the time that has lapsed since our first
introduction. Every time you look at this watch, I want it to remind
you of me; that every second should be about our time together, that
every second for me is as precious as the next. My time with you has
been so beautiful, it has been a pleasure, it has meant a lot to me –
the smiles that we have had, the joys that we have experienced. I
want Time to remind us of how we are together.

Thank you for your gesture. Thank you for what you have given me. It means a lot to me to know that you have thought of me. Every second shall always remind me of you. Every second with you will always bring joy to my heart. I cannot think of a time, when I have been with you, without those seconds... I cannot think of a time without you... This watch that you have given me, this gesture you have made, will remind me of you, always. But I do not need this watch for me to think of you, to remind me of us, to remind me of our time together. To me, I *feel* every second of my time with you. I feel you in my blood and in my bones, in my heart and in my mind, in my body and in my soul.

It is true that it is our anniversary. It is true that it is three years since we first met. It is also true that I have no present for you. If I am to be honest, then it is also true that I had not thought of it. I think of our time together, in which every second of my time with you seems like eternal joy. A joy that lets me forget that time is passing. I am forever here with you as in the first moment when we met. I am sorry that I have not remembered. I am sorry that I —

You do not have to say anything. You do not have to say a word. I do not want you to feel guilty. I do not need a present. You are a 'present' enough for me — after the worry that I have had, after the dreadful thoughts that I have thought — the thoughts that I had lost you.

I did not know what was wrong. I had no idea when they had contacted me. I did not know how serious it was. All I knew was that you were to have an emergency operation, that they were to operate before I could get to see you. It may not have been serious, but the thought of losing you was. That day, just a few months ago now, I thought of the seconds that passed – those seconds that you were in that theatre. Those seconds passed slowly, they seemed like eternity. It was then that I thought of the times we had had together, the times when there was no gap between us. It was at that time that I thought there could be an endless space between you and me, that there would be no further moments when we are as one.

They told me – they told me that you had appendicitis. They said your appendix had ruptured, that the poison from within was now in the rest of your body. When I heard that, when I realised what had happened, I felt coldness in my body. I felt loneliness.

They said that they had to operate. That there was only a whisper of time before the poison might have taken you away. A whisper... a few seconds... before you were on the edge of existence — before your life would be no longer, before the other half of me would no longer exist. Before I would no longer exist.

I imagined, I imagined the poison spreading... through your body, like some kind of infection. I thought of it spreading, spreading into your blood and then into your bones, into your heart and into your mind, through to your whole body and eventually taking away your soul.

It seemed like the infection was wanting to destroy our 'one-ness', to destroy us as we are one — to create a space between you and me. It seemed that the coldness and loneliness of death would find its way to my heart after it had consumed you. I was frightened. I was scared.

In those times, when I felt my existence threatened, I felt I could no longer live. They were the times when my breathing lost its purpose and wanted to come to an arrest.

It made me think. It made me think that should we ever die, then I would want to die first. I would want to die first and to die in your arms. I could not imagine being without you. I could not be without you. The pain would be too much.

I now know that had the operation been any more serious, I would not be happy now, that I would be in sadness. I am glad all that is left of that time is this scar, here, on your abdomen. That this scar shall represent the moments I thought I had lost you, the moments in which I was scared, those moments when the seconds went by so slowly.

It is also the scar that brought you back to me, the scar that has rescued me from being lost without you, the scar that tells me that you can no longer have this problem. It is the scar that has sealed my love for you; each side of the wound has been joined together as one — as we are one.

I thought I had lost you and I wanted you to know that every second for me shall be as precious as the previous one. That this watch that I have given you is meant for you, so that you can understand that every second of my life is with you.

I remember that time, just before my operation. I remember the pain — not the physical pain that hurt me so, but the one here in *my* heart. It was the pain of not having you nearby, the pain of not knowing where you were. Yes, I felt the coldness and loneliness in those moments, those moments without you — those moments of pain.

But it was then, when my eyes were closing, when I could not help closing them, just before I fell asleep, that I knew you would be there for me. I knew that when I awoke you would be there for me. It was like all those times when we fell asleep together.

Every second of my life is with you, too. Every second of my life is you. I do not see, feel, think or dream of anyone else. You are here in the moments I wake. You are here in the moments I sleep.

As my eyes open in the morning, I see you lying on top of me, resting your head on my chest. As my eyes open, I look down to see you, to see if you are sleeping. As I look down you turn your head towards me. It is in those moments when I wake that I see you smiling at me. It is in those moments, when I know you will be smiling at me every morning, that I know I would not want to live life without you. The seconds that pass would be nothing without that smile.

As your eyes close and succumb to sleep, I sometimes feel that I may lose you. I sometimes feel that you may never wake. That when you close your eyes as you lie here beside me, it could be the end of my life with you.

I sometimes do not want to sleep. I do not want to sleep for the fear of closing my eyes, for the fear of not seeing you again. But you give me every reason to awake. You give me every reason for my life to not end. It is the joy I look forward to — to seeing your head on me and seeing your smile as I wake.

I wish I had met you before. Even though we are young and we have our lives ahead, it still seems to me too short a time to be with you.

I wish I had this feeling some time ago. It makes me feel tearful, knowing that I have spent a part of my life without you; knowing that there were times when I could have felt this happy, that this happiness has in some way been lost. And when I think about this lost happiness I get a pain, the pain of losing something I have never had, the pain of losing something out of my reach, the pain of the past, something that I may have lost in the past.

It feels like I have been cheated, cheated by not having had you there. The past has cheated me... Time has cheated me.

Yes... yes... cheated. It was then, in those moments, that I also thought Life would cheat me. It was the time when you had that operation. They were the moments in which I held my breath. They were the moments when I could no longer breathe. It was the time when my breath was taken from me. I knew at that time when we were together that I could not exist without you. That you and I were as one. That somehow these stitches that closed up your wound should have been tied to me — that you and I should be together. We are as one, and in your breath I live and in mine you are living too. That had we been stitched together there would be no space: that the physical place where I could have been joined to you would have been in your arms. To be there until we die.

I knew when we were in hospital. I knew then. I knew that I belonged in your arms and that they were for me and for me alone.

It is your place. It is my favourite place, the place where you belong, that place which is under my arms — the place your shoulder leans into as we walk together. It is that place that holds you in a position that lets me hold you firmly; it feels natural and comfortable for you to be there. It is my favourite place: it is your place.

69

I love you. I will always love you from the bottom of my heart.

My heart is yours. It is for you to keep forever.

VIII

Your Trust

You once said something to me which was so nice, something which told me how much I meant to you. Do you remember? Do you remember the time when you were in my arms, the time as we lay next to one another, just as we are now? You told me that when we are in our space you felt that the sheet of glass between yourself and others had melted away. Do you remember?

I remember. I remember because... because I had thought something at that time. I had thought that... that when I first met you, you stood out in the crowd for me. It felt as if the world had melted away. It felt as if everything in my sight was you. That, at that time, all I could think about was kissing your tender lips. That, at that time, all I wanted to do was to caress your gentle face. You had made me feel that way. You made me feel that way because I had seen a look on your face. I had seen that expression on your face. I had seen your smile. It was that that had made the world disappear.

I remember when we first met. I remember I could not tell you exactly how I felt. I had difficulty in saying some words. But those words that you say are ours, those words we have been using, one four three, I like to say them again and again. To repeat them: one four three, one four three, one four three...

These are the words that bring joy to my heart. They are the words that I love to say. They are the words I love to hear. They are the words that roam freely in this space around us. It feels as if they can exist with me. It is as if they are a part of me. They no longer tug at me. They no longer seem to be pulling at me. They do not cause me anxiety to express them. As I am me, so these words exist. As I am me, so you exist. You and these words are a part of me. We are inseparable.

How can I ever be apart from you? How could I ever express how much you mean to me? I am who I am now only because of you: I am without those fears, I am without those fetters. It is because of you that I am happy. It is you who has provided me with my fundamental need, a need that everyone wants, a need that everyone requires — a need to be wanted. It is also you who has allowed me to mature, who has led that little boy away from that corner.

Before you, I was dead. With you, I am alive. Without you, I would have ceased to exist: I was lonely without love, I was lonely with my fears. All there was was me. Perhaps I would have collapsed into myself. Perhaps I would have been suffocated by my existence. But you are the air that I breathe. You are the life in my breath. You are the one I needed.

I cannot tell you how important your trust has been to me. I cannot tell you how much I could not trust others. It seemed that by being with me they would disappear. It seemed that by being with me they would leave me. I thought that through liking someone they would die.

I like you. You have not disappeared. You have not turned your back on me. You are here now. You have trusted me. You do not know how touched I am by you being here, how important it is for me to know that there is no space between you and me.

I was on the edge when I saw you. I was on some kind of precipice. It was your trust that kept me back. It is your trust that makes me feel that others are okay, that I am okay. It is your trust that makes me feel I can be validated as a human being, that I am worthy of being human.

There are no more edges for me to stand on. There are no more precipices. There is just you.

When I saw you, when I saw your smile, there was something inside me that gave a little flutter. There was something inside me that told me that there was something genuine about you. Something told me that that beautiful smile, those beautiful teeth your smile avails, belonged to someone who herself must be very beautiful inside. You did not know this, but it was your smile that pulled me back from the precipice.

Now, I have every opportunity to touch the face to which that smile belongs.

Sometimes when I caress your face, I wonder... I wonder what life would have been like had that little boy been caressed. Perhaps he might not have been unhappy. Perhaps I would not have been unhappy...

I am glad that you are here. I am so very glad.

Yes, I am here. Yes, I will always be here. Here for you to touch my face. To touch it as you do — so very gently, so very expressively. You touch me in a way that makes me value me, in a way that tells me you respect me, a way that tells me you love me.

These gentle hands of yours, they are so soft, they are so considerate. It makes me want to rest my cheeks in your hands. It makes me want to move them over my body.

You have also taught me something. You have taught me that I can be respected. That despite whatever I have gone through, whatever my anxieties are, I can feel safe in your hands.

When I hold your hand up in the air like this, I know every reason why I am with you. These hands that you have, they are men's hand. They are men's hands and they do not feel threatening. They are strong and sensual, ones in which I can close my eyes and feel their warmth, feel their warmth without any fear...

Do you remember this? Do you remember this gesture, this one I am making in the palm of your hand?

I remember. I remember it. I also remember the many times that you have made that gesture.

Have you noticed anything else? Have you noticed anything else about my hands?... Have you noticed the shape of my palms? Have you noticed that small inward curvature? Do you see it? It tells me that we were made for one another. It tells me that is where you also belong: that this inward curvature matches exactly that slight outward curvature of your stomach; that my palms, my hands, have their place resting upon your stomach. This is the place, the place just below where the cord sustained your life whilst you were in your birth chamber. Had it not been for that cord, my life would have been cold and lonely.

It is here where my hand can rest. It is here that it should be. When it is here it makes me feel like I have the most beautiful woman in my hands; that my hands were meant to be for you. That should you ever have the need for the operation that I had, then perhaps the stitches that will be used to close your wound could be tied to me, tied to my hands, so that you and I can be together — you under my arms, my hand upon your abdomen.

Your hand is meant to be there. I can feel its warmth travelling though my body. It gives me a warmth that flows in my blood and in my bones, that flows in my heart and in my mind, that infiltrates my body and my soul. It is a beautiful place to put your hands. It is a natural place; a place that will always be for you.

I remember how much I used to want someone to touch me. I remember how I wanted it to be meaningful. When you touch me, I feel safe. When you touch me, I feel loved. It is also nice that you have not said to me that there are other parts of me that it seems natural for your hands to belong to — I feel that you respect me.

Maybe, maybe one day, one day when we die, we will die in each other's arms: my shoulders under your arms and your hands upon my abdomen. That is how I would like us to retire from life: you and I as one.

But I fear that this may not be possible. I fear that this may not last. Whilst your hand resting upon me feels so wonderful, there is something I must say, there is something I need to say. I do not know how you will feel, but I have to say it... I am with child.

What can I say? What can I say that will express my feelings? Yes, yes, you and I will no longer be as one. Perhaps this smile and these tears that I am showing will tell you how I feel.

This child, this child of ours, I will hold it; I will hold our child ever so dearly. I will hold it in this space that is in my arms. It will be the most precious thing in my life. And it is a gift from you. What words can I say, but those that come from my heart: one four three.

Folie

IX

I Smelt the Crimson

I do not know how long it has been. I do not know how long this silence has occurred for. It has been a while. It may have been a long time. My mind has become confused — it does not want to think clearly. All I know is that it must have been since that day when you told me, that day when you came home with that expression on your face — that look of despondency.

I do not know what this silence is. I do not know what this silence means. I am not sure why we have accepted it. It seems that for everything else, we can say words. It seems that for everything else, we can maintain some semblance of communication. That that communication may not be at the level we were at before, but we are still here together as one. And it is this one-ness that tells me that we are still good for one another. It tells me that the silence cannot break us. It also tells me that we need to talk. To talk about the words we have accepted as ones which we cannot say, to talk about the words which we find difficult to say.

Sometimes I feel that as we are one, as we share the same space, that you are trying to push me away. It seems that this space I share with you makes you feel that I am too intrusive. It feels like this space we share is suffocating you. I know that you do not want to fracture this space we are in, and I know that you are not doing this intentionally. But I need you to know, to know that whilst you are not trying to push me away, I feel that you are rejecting me: rejecting me from being a part of some shared space; rejecting me for not knowing about the silence.

There are times when you look in pain. There are times when you are withdrawn. It is in those moments, those instances, that I feel trapped: trapped into wanting to talk to you; trapped into wanting you to talk to me. When I think about the words I want to say, they do not seem to come, they do not seem to form. It is as if I am paralysed: unable to speak any words, unable to think any words. And deep down, I long for you to say something to me, something that will stop me being in this confused state.

I have noticed for a while, I have noticed for some time, that when I wake up, when I open my eyes and see you lying next to me, I see that your back is turned to me. Every morning, I no longer seem to see your smile. Every morning, I no longer feel your arms around me. It seems that every day since you came home with that look in your eyes, your back has been turned towards me. It seems that every day since you came home with that look in your eyes, you sleep as if you are curled into a ball. It seems that there is no space for my arms to be placed around your waist. It is as if you do not want me to hold you. It is as if you no longer want me, as if you no longer care.

I do know what has happened. You have told me something. You have told me something that is just a description of an event. It is not the affect of it upon you. It is important for me to know what impact it has on you, although I can see some affect in you turning your back to me. It is also important for me to know how you feel it is affecting us.

This event that you have described, I shall say what it is. I shall say it not to hurt you. I shall say it not because I can cope with it but because I need to, because we need to. We need to share our feelings about your 'miscarriage'... *Our* 'miscarriage'.

I think it is time we shared our feelings. I think it is time we talked of what has remained silent. It may not be easy. It may be difficult. But by us leaving some part of our lives unattended to we would no longer be as one.

I want us to be as one. I do not want to cause a fracture between us. I had not realised that you could not find a space for your arms around my waist. I had been unaware of that. I have also been unaware that I turn my back to you every morning. It is not something I had wanted to do. I hope you can forgive me for that. I hope you do not think any less of me.

Sometimes I find it difficult to talk. Sometimes I find it overwhelming. It is as if all my emotions are running wild inside. And when they run wild, I feel helpless. I feel helpless and collapse inside. It is as if the words I want to say I cannot. It is as if the feelings that I think I am feeling are not them. It feels numb inside. I feel as if I just want to stay in my own space: a space in which I am allowed to 'be'; a space I need to create; not instead of you, but to protect myself and also to protect you.

You are the world to me and I love you. But I fear that by talking about it, by holding me, by touching me, that somehow this numbness will spread. That it will spread to you. That it will spread to us as we are one. I do not want our relationship to be like that. I do not want to have the responsibility of spreading that numbness to something as precious as you and us. It is because of this fear I have that I need this extra space. It is because of this fear I have that I should have asked you for some privacy. It is also a space in which I have not forgotten that one four three.

When you say that word, when you speak that word — 'miscarriage' — I feel pain, I feel hurt. It seems that every time I hear that word, every time it enters my ears, that the word itself becomes very painful, that the word itself is very hurtful. When I hear that word, it feels like I have been stung. It feels like a sting in my heart. It feels like a sting in my mind. It is as if it reverberates throughout my body. It is strange how words can hurt.

But it is the meaning, the meaning of that word, the sense that I make of it through my experience, that stirs some emotions in me. It stirs some emotions in waters that are already turbulent for me — it makes things more disturbing. I know it must be difficult for you to understand. I know you may not feel a part of what has happened to me. But these things do not wait for people to be together, for people to be present for one another, before they happen. I wish I had had you there at the time.

...

When I was there, when I was in L _____, I was on my own. I wasnot doing much. I was not doing anything excessive. I was just walking... just... just walking.

As I was walking, I felt a pain... I felt a pain here, in my stomach, in my abdomen. The pain — it felt... felt like I had cramp, it felt like I had some spasms... here in my stomach.

I had to rest. I thought I had to rest. I thought our baby was trying to tell me that I needed to rest. Maybe it was trying to tell me something. Maybe it was uncomfortable.

I rested. I had a rest, I did.

When I woke up... when I woke up I opened my eyes and I looked downwards... I saw blood; I saw blood between my legs. It was dark, the blood was dark. It was dark and thick and mucous-like and it was on my thighs. I was scared, I was so scared. I could see the bleeding become heavier and darker and greyish — it was grey, it was grey.

When I saw the grey, when I saw it, I knew our baby was dying. I knew it. It was the colour of death. But our baby, our baby could not speak. Our baby had no chance to speak. Perhaps it did not want to speak. Perhaps it died in fear of speaking. Maybe it was too much, too much for it to suffer — to suffer with that fear, to be paralysed by that fear. Perhaps it was too much for it to enter this world. I do not know. I do not know.

But I had this pain. I still had some pain. I could see the blood. It was still there. I saw the blood and the blood began to have clots in it, it began to have clots. I saw the blood, it was there, it was becoming brighter — I saw the crimson, I saw the crimson on my legs and I could smell it. I could smell the crimson.

I saw the crimson tears of our child and it could not speak. It could not speak but it was trying to tell me something. Those tears, those red tears, they were saying 'goodbye'. They were saying 'goodbye'...

I felt it in that moment. I felt it in that instant, the moment when life had drained from our baby... Our baby was lost.

...

I went to the clinic in L_____. I did not contact you. I could not contact you. I was afraid. I was afraid I had let you down, that I had failed you. It felt like I had failed me. I could not see you. I did not want to see you. I had death inside my birth chamber. It made me feel cold. It made me feel lonely. It made me question my existence.

When I was at the clinic, when I was there, they took out our child. They took out our child from my womb. They scraped out our baby. They scraped out our dead baby. They destroyed the cord. They destroyed the cord that provided our baby with life. They destroyed it and our baby was no longer.

I should have known something was wrong. I should have realised. I could not hear our child. I could not hear its distress... I could not save it.

...

Now, when I go to sleep, when I lie in bed, when I am in that moment of quiet before my eyes close for the night, I sometimes hear our child. I sometimes hear our child calling for help. I hear our child calling from this empty space that is inside me.

When I wake up... when I wake up every morning and look down and feel my abdomen, I feel this emptiness. It is as if it is there to remind me. It is as if it is a part of me, that I am filled with emptiness. That life is empty.

When I feel this emptiness, when I feel that some part of me is missing, I want to close this empty space that exists: to close it by bringing my knees up against my chest, to do this whilst I am in bed, to stay there in the warmth.

Something has changed. Something has changed for me. Something has changed because of this emptiness. I do not feel right. My body does not feel the same. I look at my body and I do not like it. I do not like my body because it has failed me. When I see it in the mirror, I notice that there is a distance between myself and my body. I see a failure of motherhood; I see a failure of womanhood, of me as a human being.

I could not hold my child to term. I could not hold my child in my womb. It makes me feel that some part of me as a woman is missing. It makes me feel that some part of my femininity is missing. That in some ways I am less of a woman. It makes me feel inadequate: that I cannot complete myself as a woman; that there is some kind of void in my womanhood.

Sometimes when people look at me, when others know what I have been through, sometimes I think I am less of a person. That they think I am incomplete, that in some ways they think I am not normal, that to others my femininity is questioned.

I could not talk about this to you – I could not. What would you think? What would you think of me?

I thought... I thought... I thought that if I did not talk about it, if I did not say anything, then perhaps I could stop this pain from spreading. Perhaps I could also stop the pain I receive from others: the pain of their judgements, the pain of seeing me as different. My fear of speaking was the fear of having this pain.

Even then, when I stopped my tears from showing, to stop others from seeing an 'inadequacy' in me, even then, I tried to detach myself from those tears that were flowing inside me. These tears that I have inside, they are for our child. They come from my heart. But I have to distance myself from them. I have to distance myself from our child. Otherwise I would not cope.

Perhaps I wanted to distance myself from the tears. Perhaps I wanted to detach myself from our baby. Maybe I did not care enough. Maybe I did not want to have the baby, and by not wanting to have the baby I killed it... I killed it, I killed our baby.

I am so confused. Hold me. Hold me, please.

Everything that you have said to me, everything that you have shown, tells me that *you did* care for our child, that you did *want* our child and that you would *never* have harmed it.

It is the first time you have talked to me about this. It is the first time I have begun to understand what you might be feeling since that day you came back. I want you to know that I am here for you. I want you to know that I do not think any less of you. As you and I are as one, you should have trusted me with this before. As we are as one, I want to support you. As we are as one, I love you. As we are as one, you do not have to be alone at times like this.

That emptiness you feel, the emptiness that makes you feel less of a woman, it is a feeling that tells me that you are exactly experiencing your femininity to the full. It is a space that I shall be happy to place my arms around. It is a space in which I will know that I have the woman I love in my arms.

That space will also exist as we are together. It will allow us not to forget: as we are one there will be a space with us, not a space that is *between* us, but one that is *with* us. We cannot let this space disappear — it would be as if our child had not existed. We are as one with this space.

X

It Hurts

It has been a while since we have talked. It has been a while since we have talked of the silence, since we have mentioned our miscarriage. You have supported me in that time. You have shown some understanding. I am not sure how I could have coped with life without you. You have been there for me throughout that time. You are still here for me, still providing me with support in my moments of sadness.

As I lay beside you, I felt your arms around me. I felt them holding me, telling me that you are there. I have felt your arms protect me. They have also comforted me. They make the emptiness more tolerable.

For some time now, you have placed your hands around me. For some time now you have been holding me around my waist. You have been doing this more often recently. I have also noticed that your embraces are much tighter. They feel much stronger. It seems that you are afraid of letting me go. It seems that you do not want to let me go, that you cannot let me go. It is something I have noticed. Something which I have noticed since we talked of our miscarriage.

Since that day, you have been strong for me. Since that day, I have wanted to say how much I appreciate you – that I am lucky to have someone like you. As I lay asleep in bed, there was something inside me that wanted to say those three words to you. Those three words that are private to us: one four three.

When I woke up and looked beside me, I saw an empty space. I thought you had left me. I thought you had left me because you could no longer cope with my moments of sadness. I had thought that you might not want to deal with my sadness. I was frightened. I was frightened that you had gone; that all that was left of you was the smell of your body. Something that I thought would fade away. Something that I thought would disappear, that would vanish into oblivion. No trace of you anywhere.

In that moment, in that instant, when I woke up and I did not see you lying next to me, I thought my life had ended. In that moment, in that instant, I heard you crying in the distance. The cry reminded me of my sister. She cried in the moment of her death. When I heard you cry, I also heard our child crying. She, too, must also have cried in the moment of her death.

When I saw this empty space beside me and I heard your cry, I thought you, too, had been lost, that you, too, had died. Perhaps it is just that: your crying seemed like a pain that you could not bear. And now I see you sitting here naked, curled up, in this corner; perhaps you, too, want to die.

You do not know how painful it is for me to see you like this, to see you lonely in your corner. Just as you were there for me, I will be here for you. We are as one and we, as one, cannot let this space open up between us. We cannot let the silence ruin the trust we have for one another.

This silence that you maintain – I know it is about me. I think it must be related to what we have talked about. I know it must be related to our miscarriage. In all other aspects, you have communicated with me. In all other aspects, we are as one. But since that day we talked about the miscarriage you have supported me, you have listened to me, but there is something that you are withholding, something that prevents you from being fully 'present' with me.

I am here. I am here now.

I am sorry. I am sorry that you have to see me like this. But I have been hurting, hurting for some time. This hurt that I feel, it does not seem to go away.

You are right, I do need to talk. I do need to talk to you. This pain that I feel, it *is not* about you. This pain that I feel *is* about our miscarriage. That day we talked, we talked about you. We talked about your feelings. I had to be silent, to be silent so that you could feel that I was supporting you.

I feel trapped. I feel this hurt and I feel trapped. I want to talk to you. I want to talk to you about my feelings. I want to talk about my pain. I fear that if I speak, somehow you might feel that I am lessening the value of your words, lessening the value of your feelings. That somehow you might feel that, by talking about my feelings, it might mean that mine are more important than yours. I do not want you to feel that I am taking away the importance of your feelings. But I need you to acknowledge the importance of mine.

Sometimes, I feel that, as a man, I am not allowed to have these feelings. That, as a man, I am not supposed to have these feelings. That it should be impossible for me to have them. That I have no right to feel the way I do. But I am also human, a human being with emotions. I cannot continue to put aside my feelings.

I am angry. I am angry at the world. I am angry because the whole world sympathises with *you*. I am angry because I am left in this corner with no importance other than to support you.

There are no pictures, no details and no trace of our baby's life anywhere, no trace. Just an image in my mind of a perfect baby, no longer in your birth chamber, no longer in this world, but still alive here in my heart. I cannot touch, I cannot hold, but our child is alive somewhere.

I do not know what is happening. I know something is not right. When I lie beside you and your eyes are closed to the world, it is then, at night, when I seem to get restless. You do not see it. You cannot see it, but at times... sometimes I get numbness in my arms, first one then the other. And at times, I get numbness in my legs. When things inside me are not clear, when thoughts rush through my head, I get an uneasiness that keeps me awake. My head, my head starts to feel numb. I think these thoughts; I think they want me to feel numb. When I worry, when I worry about these thoughts, the numbness spreads. It spreads down my back. I do not know what it is but I get out of bed. I get out of bed and sit in this corner. Sit in this corner before my heart becomes numb. Sit in this corner before I lose all sense of my feelings.

Somehow, I think it might be my fault. Perhaps I feel guilty. Perhaps I feel guilty at not having protected you: guilty for not being there with you when it happened; guilty for not being there for my child. I know I have no control over what happens in your birth chamber, but this is how I feel.

I ask myself at times. I ask myself if there was anything I could have said or done that could have kept our child alive. Perhaps I had hurt you. Perhaps had we not been in union whilst you were with child. Perhaps it was in our union that our child was hurt, that our child was damaged. In our joy, in our shudder, the instant where we expressed our love for one another, perhaps it was then that our love, our need for congress, to be in union, perhaps it was then that love through sex led to death. That loving and sex are like death. Perhaps it was in our congress that we lost our child.

I do not know. I do not know. I am just trying to find ways to understand. I am just trying to find ways to understand what has happened. It is as if there is some void — a void in not knowing how it could have happened. It is as if there is a void in thinking about ways in which I could have prevented it from happening. It is a void I cannot fill.

I also feel a void here, inside. It is a void about not knowing. It is a void about my past. It is a void about my future. It is a void that I could have healed.

That boy who was lonely, that boy who would prefer to withdraw into himself rather than meet other people, that boy who would rather die than speak, that boy who every time he got to know somebody thought they would die — it is that boy who is now a man who is still hurting. It is something that has not disappeared from my life. It is a pain that makes me who I am. It is there somewhere, hidden away.

When I was younger, when I was a boy, I used to think that when I became a father I could protect my child, that I could comfort my child, prevent those things that had happened to me. I used to think how I could raise my child to not be afraid. I used to think about how I could raise my child to be loved. How by making my child's life much better than mine I could heal this little boy inside me, knowing that my child would not be lost in this world.

Because I cannot turn back time, because I cannot undo the things that were done to me, I could at least hold this little boy, hold my child, let him know, let him know that I was there, that I had not forgotten him, that he was never alone. But my arms can no longer hold our child. My arms can no longer hold this little boy. They seem to get numb. They seem to get numb with an empty space. And it hurts; it hurts because that little boy remains in the fetters of his existence.

As a man, I look back at that boy and I see some distance between him and me. A distance that I thought I could close. It is that distance that is the void. The void I wanted to fill.

When the miscarriage occurred I was not there. I was at a distance — a distance in which I was not there for you. Another distance I could do nothing about. But I am left with these feelings about *our* child, not about this boy inside, but *our* child: a father's feelings, a father's love — gone... ripped from my heart. Not even a moment, not even an instant, to save our child.

It hurts. It hurts so much. It hurts here in my stomach.

I no longer want to be strong for you. I no longer want to be strong for the world. I just want to be acknowledged, not as a man, but as someone who has lost a child and who happens to be a man.

I looked to you for support. I looked to you to be strong for me. In all this time, I have not thought about what it must have been like for <u>you</u>. In all this time I have not thought about your needs. I have focused on mine. I have become detached from you.

One of the things that I admired about you when we first met was your sensitivity, your gentleness. The other was that you risked everything in talking to me. I saw courage and fortitude that made me think that you were amazing. You were also courageous for me. It seems that since that day I came back, you have shown nothing but those same qualities that I admired. Even with your fears and your anxieties, you put me first.

The words that you have spoken, they do not lessen the value of my feelings. Those words that you have spoken comfort me in knowing that I am not alone. They are like arms that are wrapped around me.

I do not know what it means to be a man. I cannot pretend that I do. But I can understand the need to protect our child. I understand the helplessness when there is something not in your control. A miscarriage happened and I am sure, in every cell of my being, that could you have prevented it you would have done so. You would have done so whether or not you are a man. It is in your caring that it is so. You would have done so because of your love for our child. I see the full expression of your masculinity in the tears that you show, in the pain that you feel. And I have not disappeared from your sight.

That void between the little boy and you — it is not so large, it is not so distant as you think. We, too, have our lives. We, too, can try again. We, too, can be with child. Perhaps when that happens then you, I, our child and that little boy can be as one.

XI

An Illusion

Is there something you would like to tell me?

No.

Is there something you would like to share with me? Something that you feel I may need to know?

I do not understand why you are asking me these things. I do not understand why you are talking to me in this way. It is clear to me that something is of concern to you. It is clear to me that something is making you feel angry. From the way you ask me these questions, I think you feel that I have done something – something that you have found offensive.

Is there something you would like to tell me? Is there something I should know?

I do not know what you are talking about. I do not know what you mean. How can I talk to you when I do not know what you refer to? Perhaps you would like me to say something. Perhaps you would like me to say something that will confirm your anger, something that you want to attribute to me.

I would like you to tell me the truth. I would like to know the truth. You and I are as one and as we are one, we cannot have any untruths between us. We cannot have any untruths because of the fractures they may cause, the fractures that may cause a space between us. I think I can see a fracture, but I need you not to confirm it. I need you to tell me it is an illusion. And if it is not an illusion, then I would like you to respect me, to respect me as being a part of your shared space and to tell me, to tell me because we have shared our smiles.

I do not know what you expect me to say. I do not have anything to say. You are frightening me. What is it that you see? What is it that you think you see?

Maybe I see a distance emerging. Maybe I feel the world around me is not nice again. All I wanted was to trust someone. All I ask for is to be trusted. Can trust ever exist without the truth?

I am not here to frighten you. I am not here to make you feel awkward. I am here because I do not want to be frightened by the truth any more. I am here because whatever little space that may have developed between us, I would like to close it. I would like to close it because of my implicit trust in you, because of my implicit trust in 'us', and it can only be closed by the expression of truth.

I do feel angry. I do feel angry inside. Angry because I think my view of reality has shifted, that my view is clouded by an illusion, and for me to remove that illusion I need you to be honest with me. There is nothing in this world that would make me not want to be with you. There is nothing so awful that we as one cannot overcome it. If you love me as I love you, then you must be honest with me; you must tell me the truth, no matter how difficult it may be for you. You must tell me the truth.

I do not think you are well. I have no idea what you are referring to.

I know.

If there is anything you feel I have mislead you about —

I KNOW.

What do you know? Tell me.

You know that I have had difficulties in accepting the loss of our child. You know that I have not been able to cope. You saw me lose weight. You saw me not maintaining my hygiene. You saw that I became disinterested in life. You heard my voice fade away. You heard it fade into a murmur. You heard my cries at night as I sat lonely in the corner. You had heard that life had all but left my breath. I could not live like that for you. I could not live like that for us.

I kept seeing our child. I kept seeing our child in this space next to me as I woke. I saw our child's face and head. I saw our child's arms and legs. It is as if there is some form of emptiness within 'us'. It is like an empty space that cannot be fulfilled. It is something that reminds me that I am lonely, something that also makes me 'me' and you 'you'. It is something that I feel that does not make us as one. When I wake, I see our child, but I do not see 'us'. In that moment, in that instant when I wake up, I see a distance between us. It is this gap that has shaken the core of my humanity; my humanity seems to be about my loneliness; my humanity is loneliness.

It is because of these thoughts. It is because of these feelings that I wanted to be with you. I wanted us. I wanted us to live life to the full again: in my blood and in my bones, in my heart and in my mind, in my body and in my soul. I wanted... I wanted to find some help for me. I wanted... I wanted to do this so that I could love you as I have done, to love like no other.

I did not know what to do. I had to look for help. I did not know where to go. All I could think about was where you had gone for help: how they nursed you; how they must know how to help me.

No!

I contacted that clinic, that clinic in L_____.

No!

I told them I needed help. I told them your name. I told them when you were there.

Oh, darling!

They asked me for your date of birth.

I am sorry!

I told them I could not cope. I told them I could not cope with our loss, that I did not know how to help you.

I am so sorry!

Then they told me... they told me... they told me you had been there... but... but... they only performed abortions.

Forgive me!

They said they do not handle miscarriages; that miscarriages go to a local hospital in another town.

Darling, forgive me, pl–

They told me that their licensing only allows them to conduct abortions and that there were no other clinics in L_____.

I am so, so, sorry!

Why did you *lie*? Why did you *lie to me*?

Where do I begin? How do I start? I... I... I do not know if anything I could say would help you understand. I do not know if anything I could say would allow you to forgive me. But I need to let you know that there were times when I had no choice, that there were times when it was the only way. You may not agree but I did this for 'us'. I did this so that I could be with you, so that I could live life to the full with you — because we as one is all that needs to be.

This foetus that was inside me, this foetus which was inside my birth chamber – I felt it drained blood from me. It was as if I were dying. It was as if death was catching up with me. It was like before. It was just like before, with my twin... I had to survive, I had to... I know now, I know now, given that you are in my blood and on my bones, in my heart and in my mind, in my body and in my soul, I know I did not want to be without you. I had to survive, I had to. Do I lose my life and lose you, or do I lose a child... When death is growing inside, what can you do?

Stop these lies, stop them. You killed our baby!

The foetus was only twenty weeks old.

Foetus! Foetus! You want to tell me now it was a foetus! You were *with child*, you were *not with foetus*!

When you talked of our miscarriage we had lost our *'baby'*, our *'child.'* Now you come to me about your abortion and we now have a *'foetus'*. Is this what you want to do to me, play mind games? Is this what you did to me to make me feel sorry for you when you talked about our miscarriage? Is this what you are doing to ease your conscience: to shed some degree of responsibility over our child by calling it a 'foetus' when you wanted an abortion? Perhaps you want to detach yourself from calling it a 'baby': maybe this is how cold you really are.

The whole world can be sympathetic to you when you lose *a baby* of twenty weeks. The whole world can turn their heads away when you destroy *a foetus* of twenty weeks. But I will not turn my head away just so that you do not have to think about what you did to our baby.

Did you think about me? Did you think about me at all? Did you not care for me?

Of course I care for you. Of course I love you.

Then why?!

Do you remember that time, the time that I told you I was pregnant? Do you remember? In that moment when we were in each other's arms, you had told me that I was in your blood and in your bones. It meant everything to me. We were as 'one'. There was no fear of losing you, no fear of losing you like I had my sister. We were together. We were like twins in our relationship.

As I was born... my mother... my mother... she tried to suffocate me, she tried to stop me from breathing. I think she did this because I had killed my sister: my mother − I do not think she has forgiven me. It was as if she had rejected me, as if I was no longer wanted; it compounded my loneliness.

You said to me as we were with one another, as we were holding each other, you said to me that I was in your blood and in your bones. For the first time, for the first time, I felt complete − as a person, as a woman, as a partner. For the first time I truly felt happiness.

But then you said something else. You said something that caused me deep pain. It felt like I had been ripped in half, something that shook me to my very foundations. Something that I could not talk to you about − I was afraid to speak. I was afraid because of the feelings that I had.

These words I have are difficult to express. It seems like something that is so precious to me would be insignificant to you, that you could brush it to one side. I fear that my feelings may not matter to you, and because my feelings do not matter that, somehow, I do not matter − that I then become insignificant.

It is that insignificance that I heard. It is the rejection of me that I also heard. A rejection of me being in your world, a rejection of me as we are one, a rejection of that happiness I felt when we were together in each other's arms.

You said those words which meant that my moments of true happiness lasted a few seconds. You said those words that made me feel rejected. You said those words that made me feel lost again. Lost without 'us'. Lost without us as 'one'. Lost without our 'one-ness'.

You said our child would be... would be... 'the most precious thing in your life'. And when you said those words, I was no longer first in your heart and in your mind. I was no longer first. It felt as if you had rejected me, just like my mother had... because of a baby in a womb.

Your affections, your heart and mind, would have been with our child and not me. Your love, time and attention would have been with our child and not me. I would have been deprived by our child of all those things, of everything that that moment of happiness had meant to me — especially after a lifetime of searching. How could I let that happen? How could the life be drained away from me? This child inside me was draining the blood from me and it would have continued to drain more and more life out of me. Our child as it grew would have drained your affections, the need for my existence, away from me... just like my sister... I could not let it happen.

You killed our baby because you wanted attention! Because you are selfish!

Your words are so ugly at times.

The deeds that you have done are more so.

You have said to me that you love me. You have lied to me by not telling me in the first instance. You then lied to me by trying to conceal this original lie. But they are lies that hurt, lies that wound, lies that cause much pain. These lies that you say — these are the lies that women say, these are the lies that break men's hearts, and you have broken mine.

They may be lies that women say to protect themselves, they may be an aid to prevent the loss of love or departure of the other, but they are not truths about love. They are lies that you have said so that I will remain with you, so that you can maintain some form of unconditional love from me. They are lies that prevent you from being unloved, to prevent you from losing a love — a love that forms a part of you, which forms a part of your very being. It is a love that seems to be a validation of you as a person, a person who can be loved and is of some value.

It feels like when you said you loved me, you did not love me for me but for what I provide for you. I do not seem to be wanted for myself but am wanted to meet your inner need, for your self-esteem. It now appears that the quality I bring is not the quality of who I am but what you can use for your happiness. I can no longer believe that you can love me for me.

I cannot stay here with you just to supply you with your needs. That passion, that intensity which you once said I supply, I can no longer provide. You have not taken my needs into account.

You do not seem to understand how important you are to me. You are in my blood and in my bones, in my mind and soul, and in every second of my life I was breathing you. You do not seem to understand that a whisper, that a smile would compel me to you. At every touch, at every kiss, every smile I would tremble inside. How could I want to lose that? How can you not understand that I had to lie?

You lied to me. It was not a small lie. It was a big lie. A lie to deceive me. You lied to mislead me. You used lies to make me feel sorry for you. You used me to serve your lie. You used my emotions to cover up your lie. You do not know how much you have hurt me. You do not know how much you have crushed me. You lied and made me feel a certain way. A way that was not nice. You lied to make me feel not nice. How could you do that? How could you do that to me? I am your partner and you did not care about me. You lied to me and I cannot forgive you for that.

How can I trust you? How will I know that you will not lie to me again? How do I now know whether you have ever told the truth? The words that come out of your mouth are now meaningless. They have lost their meaning. The words that were once concrete to me are now like shadows. They have become vague. They might even have been an illusion. They were an illusion. Perhaps you are now an illusion.

You have become something that is false — a lie to the world. A lie that shows the world something you are not: a lie that is you. A lie that detracts from the truth: something that is false, something that is cheap, something to cover up what is beneath.

You have lied to me. You have lied to 'us'. You want 'us', but you accept a lie to sustain us. That is wrong. That is unfair.

What are you now — the lie or the constructor of lies? How can I know? I do not even know which is worse. What I do know, though, is that you are a destroyer of certainties: my certainty; our certainty.

...

You said to me once that you heard your sister's last cry of pain. You said you heard this in the birth chamber — the cry came as the reduced blood supply could not sustain her life. If you could hear the cry of your sister, can you imagine the cry of our baby? The cries as our baby's legs were ripped off. The cries as our baby's arms were ripped off.

Stop it!

Can you imagine that pain — the pain of having your arms ripped off, torn away?

Stop it!

Stop it!? Stop it!? But that is what they do. That is what they did to our baby. *You were informed of that, they did tell you that?* How else do you think they destroy our baby? How else can they get a twenty week old baby out of your birth chamber through your birth canal? How else do you think they do it?

Our baby... our baby had a heartbeat! Our baby had started to kick! Our baby moved around. Our baby *had its HEAD CRUSHED* and its *SPINE BROKEN.*

Stop! Please, stop!

You heard the cry of your sister. You must have heard the cry of our baby.

You have lied to me about the abortion. You have lied to me by informing me about a miscarriage. How do I know the story of your sister is not a lie?

No, no, my sister — that is true. It's —

How do I know anything you have said to me is not a lie: those one four threes, that smile? It makes me sick. It makes me sick thinking about it.

...

When we first met, all that time ago... did you tell me about your sister so that I would feel sorry for you, so that I would feel sympathy for you?

.

No, no, <u>that is true</u>. I have only wanted you —

You are lost in lies.

There are things that you must realise. There are things that you must learn to accept. I have pain, bad pain, emotional pain, psychological scars that are hurting. I cannot help what I did, the lies that I told, nor why I did it. But I cannot stop thinking about things; about the abortion, about my past, and the only way I can deal with it was to say things, say things that hid the truth, hid the pain — the pain of my past.

If I cannot hide this pain, if I feel that the pain is too much to live with, that I will be suffocated by it, then I should have the ability to decide if I want to lose my life by being asphyxiated by my past, or if I want to be with you. I lied because it is you who I wanted to be with. Had the child been born, I would have lost you, I would have lost my life and returned to that suffocation, and that is too much for me to bear. You must understand that whilst you mean the world to me, I have to decide whether I want to lose you or whether I should lose our child. It is I alone who has to decide that. It is my fear. It is my body. It is my life. It must be my right.

Right!... Yes, you have that *right*. You have that *RIGHT*. You also have the *right* to sanction someone to kill *our child*. You have the *right* to sanction someone to insert some *metal toothed forceps* inside your birth chamber; for that person to clasp our baby's *limbs* with the forceps and to pull them apart, one after the other. You have the right to say *YES* to someone *crushing* our baby's skull. You have —

Stop, please, stop!

You have the right to say YES to someone *breaking* our baby's spine—

Stop! Stop! Stop! —

You have that right. YOU HAVE THAT RIGHT —

<u>*It was a word*</u>*.*

Sorry!

It was <u>*only*</u> *a word.*

What was?

'Abortion'... It was just a word... It was something that happens down there... A word you use, not something you know about... It was something I had done... It was something I could turn my head away from... It was like a black box — I did not need to know what was inside. I did not need to know what happens. It was a box called abortion... that is all it was... it was something that happens down there... Just a word.

A word... Just like 'trust'... Just like 'us'... Just like 'love'... Something you could lie to yourself about for the rest of your life.

...

This is not about rights. This is about lies and the choices you made.

You chose to destroy our child. You chose not to keep it. *It was you* who decided it. *It is you* who has to live with that decision. *It is you* who has to live with the consequences of your choice. Your choice was just that — *your choice*: the choice that you made with the freedom to decide upon matters. You chose to sanction the death of our baby.

You have a right to make that choice. You have a right to do that and to live by the consequences.

...

Do you love me? Do you love me? As we are as one, we love one another. As we are as one and if I were to die, how would you feel? How would you feel? If you were to die I would be devastated... devastated... Yet I am not born to you. My feelings for you are not of any physical dependency, yet I have this bond to you, as you have to me. As I have this bond, I also have one to our child, our child who is not physically born to me. Just as my love for you is real, my love for my child is too.

You felt that I had no opinion, or that I should not have an opinion, that my thoughts or feelings should not influence your decision. You chose, but you did so by not wanting to hear me.

In some ways you devalued my feelings; you devalued me somehow we were no longer as one, we were two who were just together. We were two and you sought to devalue the other; you created a space between us, a space that I had not wanted. You did this out of your freedom of choice; you freely chose to disrespect me, to disrespect us who were as one, to cause a fracture between us, to cause a fracture between us now and the happiness we had.

In many ways you are right. It cannot be my choice. But you must realise that I have a choice. A choice based on what you have done, based on the consequences of your choice.

You thought about yourself. You thought about the choices that you had to make. You must have thought about the impact of those choices, the consequences of those decisions. When you had decided, you must have felt that the repercussions were acceptable to you. But I do not think that you had thought about the impact of those consequences on 'us', to us as we are one. And you did not think about the impact it would have on me.

I have a choice to hold you or comfort you. I have a choice to laugh or to cry. I also have the choice to react to what you have done, and my choice would be based on how I feel. That choice is mine and mine alone and I may choose to stay here with you. I... I may... I may choose to not want to be with you. Whatever I decide, I will decide for my reasons. Reasons that I feel I have a *right* to have, reasons that are personal to me.

You denied yourself a chance of motherhood. I did not deny myself fatherhood. It was you who denied me my fatherhood. You destroyed that part of me that makes me a man, that part of my very being that is a man — you took away my experience of being a father. You inflicted something on me without my consent. And by doing that you destroyed the trust I had in you. And you know how much trust means to me.

XII

I Felt It

I felt it in your touch. I felt it in the way your hands sought their way around my body. I felt it in the way they expressed themselves. I felt their tenderness as they travelled down toward my triangle. I looked at you as your hands rested upon their destination. I looked at you and I saw that something was on your mind. But your hands continued to impart their meaning. You allowed them to convey themselves in a manner which placed my needs above your thoughtful concerns. It was then – when your hands covered my sex with their warmth – it was then when I looked at you and smiled.

I had also felt it, before, in the shudder of your body, the moment when you and I were as one, the moment when our concerns about life suspended themselves. I felt it in that moment when our lives seemed to pass us in one gentle exhale. It felt as if that moment would last a lifetime, a lifetime in which we had secured our innermost need. I felt it reverberate throughout my body. It left a trail of goosebumps upon my skin whilst my nipples stood erect.

It was then, in that moment, in that instance, with the shudder of your body, that it felt as if the fetters of our existences unshackled;

that when we were set free, our quiet cry of joy echoed around us, an echo that filled the space that we occupied. It was then, in that instant, that we both closed our eyes; closed them so that we could shore up whatever space lay between us. In that instant, when our eyes were closed, we were locked forever in time. Locked in that moment when we understood one another.

I also felt your tears. I also felt them fall upon my breasts. They fell in the moment of your cry.

The coldness of your tears made me open my eyes. They opened to see your face. They opened to see something that I am sure I did not want to see. I saw some pain trickle out of your eyes.

It was as if that pain was desperate to escape, trying to seek its freedom as we sought ours.

Your tears fell to the comfort of my bosom. They fell as if they were trying to seek refuge. They slid down my cleavage, sliding towards my navel, arresting at a point short of being above my womb. It seems as if they feared to go any further. It seems as if it was too painful for them to go any further.

I felt it in the moment, the moment in which we suspended our breathing. It was in that moment, when our bodies gently trembled, the moment in which we needed one another, that we became unaware of the space we occupied. I felt it reverberate throughout my body, leaving a trail of goosebumps upon my skin as your sex stood erect inside.

It was then that you expressed yourself, spilling yourself inside:

your pain announcing itself in our congress.

I thought about your pain. I thought about it as we were in union, when we were as one. Perhaps it needed to show itself because of the joy of our closeness. Perhaps it needed to show itself because of the realisation that as we are one we are no longer lost. But something inside, something I cannot describe, perhaps it is a part of my very being, a part of my existence, something which is trying to communicate with me, something told me for the first time that things had changed.

I know something has changed. It feels as if there may be sadness, that there may be some regret, perhaps some anger that you cannot express. Perhaps it is about me. Perhaps it is something I have done... Is it about the words I have said? Is it the lie I have told?... I do not know.

What I do know is that you no longer seem to talk to me, talk to me in a way that would merit my counsel, in a way that shows you respect me, in a way that shows you respect 'us'. It seems that you no longer <u>want</u> to talk to me. It is as if it has become difficult for you to speak. It is as if it has become difficult for you to say anything.

I can only guess as to why you cannot talk to me, but I believe you are angry. I know that you are angry. I know that you are angry with me. I know that you have been angry with me for some time. But what I do not know is how long this can go on for. How long can this anger continue? How long will you allow it to continue? How long will you allow it to continue without talking to me?

It is not nice being in congress and seeing tears in your eyes, tears that express a pain. It is not nice being in congress and feeling something is not quite right. I would like you to talk to me. I need you to talk to me. Talk to me so that I may understand what you may be feeling, so that I can understand what you may be thinking. Talk to me... Talk to me, please.

The taste of your sex seems so different. It is no longer sweet. It is *bitter*.

Oh darling! You are angry. You are still very angry at me. It was in the past and I have hurt you. I have hurt you very much. The look on your face and the words from your mouth — the words that bridge this space between us — they tell me everything. They tell me that you look at me with rage, that you look at me with hate. They tell me that you are seething, that you are seething at me.

I know these expressions. These are expressions of the deep pain that you feel — the pain that I have caused. They leave your face looking drained. They leave your face motionless.

I also felt it. I also felt it in that moment, the moment when my sex was inside yours. I felt it in the shudder of *your* body when your sex clung onto mine, squeezing me gently, shoring up the space that was between us.

122

I had also felt it before. I felt it before when my hands covered your sex, when my hands sought to express themselves. It felt as if your sex had closed itself, that it had closed itself because it had not wanted to receive the feelings that it so desperately needed. Perhaps my hands were not as tender as before. Perhaps they were too afraid to speak for themselves. Maybe they could not convey their emotions.

You must realise that at times when I do not share your body, when I do not let you share my body, or when I am unable to share it fully, there may be emotional reasons. That these reasons upset the harmony that exists inside me: reasons that prevent me from being fully 'present' when we are entwined; reasons that prevent me from being physical with you. These reasons are my emotions, the emotions that are personal to me, the emotions that I have entrusted to you, the emotions that make us 'us'.

You must realise that when I do desire you, I desire you for emotional reasons. That it is not a purely physical act for me. These emotions that I share with you are what unite us in that moment of congress. The emotions that I share with you are also here, in my heart, when I am with you.

These last few times that we have been together – these last few times that we shared our bodies, the times when we closed that physical space that exists between us – things have felt different. They have felt different when our bodies are as one. They have felt different when we closed this space between us. I have not told you this before. I could not have told you this. I did not know how to tell you this.

I thought it would pass. It has not.

Before... some time ago... when we were as one... it seemed like we had bridged a gap, that we had closed the space that was between us. Now, it feels like we are capturing that moment when I am me and you are you. Now there seems to be a space between us, a space that is distancing me from you.

I also saw something in your eyes. I saw something that reminded me of when I was younger... As I looked at you, I saw some distance in your eyes. It was an equal distance that was reflected from my eyes.

I felt it in that moment, in the shudder of your body, the point at which our breathing suspended itself for an instant. I felt it in that moment when your sex clung onto mine, when our eyes then closed, trying to shore up that space between us. I felt your sex express its tenderness. That tenderness seemed different. Something that I had not experienced. Your sex had expressed its tenderness and the tenderness had become cold.

It was at that point, the point when your sex was clinging onto mine, the point when our bodies gently trembled. It seems it was then that your sex clung to avoid the loneliness: a loneliness which it seemed afraid of. It felt as if your sex had to fill the emptiness, the emptiness left by the void. The one that was created by its trauma.

As we are in union, I am closest to that place where you

destroyed our child. That place where he or she last lived, the place of destruction — the destruction of our child. It is also the place — because of your lie — it is also the place of destruction... of... of... of me.

You say that my tears were afraid to go any further. You say that it might be too painful for them. Perhaps they could not trust enough to go to their destination. Perhaps they did not want to go any further. Maybe something told them that should they reach their destination they would fade away into oblivion, that they would fade out of existence. That somehow they would be destroyed.

But you have destroyed some of the trust that I had in you. You have destroyed some of the feelings that I had for you. It is as if a part of me has died, as if a part of us has died. That intimacy with you no longer has those emotions that I refer to, the emotions that I entrusted to you.

When we are in that moment, the moment when we are united, some of the feelings that I had for you are lost; those feelings may have been destroyed, some of them may have died.

When we are in that moment, that instant when we are in congress, I am at a point at which I am closest to your birth chamber. That chamber where life in its infancy is nurtured. That birth chamber that has also been so destructive. It is also the point at which I am closest to where death has occurred — the place which is now a death chamber.

When we are together, when we are in union, it feels as if I have been infected by your death, your need for destruction. I am there, at that point, with you physically, but your infection has caused some of my emotions to die. I no longer feel that I am there with you — I am with you in this act, but with dying emotions. Because of you, sex has become meaningless.

It has been happening for some time now: the difficulties in sharing those moments with you. For some time, it has taken longer for you to get aroused. For some time, your sex has increasingly resisted us seeking those moments when we are as one. For some time, your sex has been increasingly reluctant to express itself by showing its tenderness — that tenderness that helps bring us together. And for some time, your sex has been increasingly dry when I am here with you.

It is as if death is creeping out of your death chamber and spilling itself onto your sex.

It seems like this infection that you have is spreading. You have destroyed our child. You have destroyed the meaning of sex. You have destroyed some of my emotions. You have destroyed our relationship.

It is not just that sex is meaningless — it is as if our relationship is meaningless, as if our relationship has become dry. It is as if my emotions are meaningless to you, as if I am meaningless.

This disease that you have... It must stop.

It is true that I have destroyed our child. It is true that I have destroyed my twin. It is true that I am destroying us. I can see that it is also true that I am destroying you. But it is also true that you are not very nice to me. You are very hurtful. I cannot forgive you. I cannot forgive you for the things that you have said.

I do not seek your forgiveness. I do not ask for it. It is not you who should be forgiving.

I do not understand why women feel that they are victims of everything. That even through their own actions, even through the unexpected consequences of their action, they seem to be the victims. It is as if it is everyone else's fault. It is as if you cannot take responsibility. That if you feel some form of sadness, that if you feel affronted, I should somehow feel some sympathy for you.

I feel something — I feel the pain. I feel the pain and I cannot let it go. Every time I look at you all I see is the grief that I experience — you have become that grief.

There are some things inside. There are some things I cannot get out of my head, things I need to say. Perhaps it may not be the right time. Perhaps the right time may never come. But what I have to say I mean from the bottom of my heart. This is what I feel and what I think. And what I have to say is not about the immediacy of this moment, is not about the immediacy of my thoughts. It is about something I have been trying to resolve for some time. It is about what has invaded my body and my soul. It is something that has flooded my heart and my mind. That has spread through my blood and my bones.

This bridge that is between us, those words that formed that bridge, the bridge between my heart and yours... is crumbling... I am not sure if I will get over these feelings... I am not sure if there are any words that will support or rebuild this bridge... Those words now seem to be like debris, falling into waters that are still for me. They seem to be causing ripples. They seem to be causing the water to become murky, causing the sediments to become unsettled, causing me much pain.

It is for those reasons that I want to say some words — they may be a few in number, but I have to say them. These words that I have, they are... are for you. They... they... come from my... my... heart... 'I do not think we have a future together'.

XIII

The Café

I know that you cannot hear what I want to say. I know that you cannot hear the thoughts that I am thinking. But our opportunity to discuss our relationship has just passed. It has passed and yet I have so much to say, so much I want you to hear. As I look into this café window, I leave you inside. I had hoped that you would look at me. I had hoped that you would give me some sign. That you would give me some signal of hope, of some desire indicating that you did not want me to go. I would have turned around and come back to you, had you given me that.

I looked around and all I could see through the window was you having turned your head away from me. Your head was looking down as you tried to reach into your bag. Perhaps you could not wait for me to go so that you could take your address book out to find someone else to talk to. Perhaps your make-up was more important to you than giving me the courtesy of a final look. It was as if you no longer had any concerns for me. It was as if you did not care that I was leaving. I felt as if I no longer existed for you. That somehow you were like the others — you looked away from me, you wanted to disappear from my life.

I know that you cannot hear what I am going to say, but I shall say these words anyway. I need to say them because of what I feel, because of this space that is between us. I need to say them because somehow, by expressing myself, even though our time has passed, I can at least imagine you listening to them. There are words which I hope will linger in this space between us, linger until your ears receive them. It may not be soon. It may never be. I want to say them just for the possibility.

I remember the nine words I said to you. They were not easy for me to say. I saw the impact of those words. I saw the impact on you as those words travelled from my mouth and floated into your ears. They were words, just words, each individual one so harmless, each individual one like a delicate sigh, like a shallow breath that we once shared. I remember those words, the moment they reached your ears; I saw a look upon your face that I did not ever want to see: I saw a woman devastated by the accumulation of some gentle sighs.

I also remember the anxiety and fear that I had when those words left my mouth. I remember how those words had to struggle to come out. As I was saying them, it felt as if I was gasping with my last breath; that in my struggle to survive, in my struggle to keep alive, that those last few gasps of air had formed those words that would allow me a few more moments of life. It was as if either those words or life itself had to escape from my body. That if I had not expressed those words, then life itself would have left me.

It may have only been two months ago, but I remember those words. Those words, they floated in this space between us; they were expressions of my life. Maybe, had I not said anything; maybe, had I not spoken those words, then my eyes would have closed themselves never to have seen your face again.

It was in this struggle, this struggle for life, that my heart had to speak. It had to find its way towards you. It had to find a way of letting you know how much pain there had been, it had to let you know how much I was drowning, how much it was suffocating with the hurt that it felt.

Every part of me wanted to be with you. Every part of me could not deal with the hurt, with the confusion, with the anger I felt. Every part of me was dying. To be with you would be like drowning in pain, suffocating into death. But you are the one that I love, and in loving you I was dying.

My need to live, my need to survive, seems to have devastated you, seems to have caused some kind of trauma that you did not expect. In the struggle for my life, I may have caused your death.

You hurt me. You hurt me in a way that I did not want you to. I wanted you to do something. I wanted you to know I wanted you to do something. You were not to know, but you hurt me.

I wanted to see you turn around, to turn around and look at me, as I sat at the table in the café. I wanted to see if I had meant anything to you. I wanted to see if there was any last semblance of feeling for me. You did not turn around. You continued to walk out the door of the café. You continued to hurt me.

Had you turned around, you would have seen me looking at you, hoping that you would stay. But as you approached that door, it felt as if I would lose you forever, that we could no longer be as one, that there was no possibility for us to be as one. As you approached the door, you did not see the tears in my eyes. You did not see that I was crying out for you. You did not see the pain I felt. It was as if the colours of the world were disappearing. It was as if my heart was becoming heavy.

I reached into my bag so that I could find something to wipe away the tears, to wipe away the tears that would otherwise have obscured my face. I wanted you to see me. I wanted you to look at me, to see my face without the expression of sadness, without the expression of pain. I wanted to prepare my face just in case you turned around. I wanted to prepare my face so that I could smile at you, should you have turned around.

By the time I had cleared my face of those tears, you had walked out of that door. You had also walked past the café shop front, walking past the window. I saw the last glimpse of the back of your coat as you walked away, disappearing past the café window. It was as if a part of me died. It was as if that sheet of glass had reappeared, as if something inside had become empty.

Once you had disappeared, once you had left, my breath stood still for a moment, my breath stood still for an instant. Once you had left, there were words wanting to escape from my mouth, words that I wanted you to hear. There were words wanting to seek your heart. These words needed to be spoken. These words needed to be said. And when my head tilted, looking downwards to one side, and my eyes began to close, it was then that the words I had to say were breathed.

These words that I uttered, these words that I breathed, they fell into this open space in front of me, a space that no longer seems to be between us — a space that seemed to surround me. It is a space in which these words are allowed to die, to fade away into some kind of oblivion.

It is sad for me to know that these words will last for only a few seconds. It is sad for me to know that they will be there for the few moments of my breath, those few moments that supply me with life. They will have at least lasted for the duration of my heartbeat. These words that I said, they are few in number but I hope they will linger in this open space until they fall into your ears... 'I would like you to come back to me'.

I wanted to hear your voice. I wanted it to fill this space. I wanted it to call me back. I wanted you to call me back. I wanted to know there was some part of you that still wanted me, some part that might still remotely like me. I wanted to know if some part of your blood, your bones, your 'being', wanted to reach out for me. I wanted to hear it desperately, even the tiniest of whispers would have made me turn around — it would have meant that you were screaming for me.

Those words that would have come from your mouth – they would have carried themselves across this space that is between us. This is the space that I wanted to close. This is the space in which those words would have told me that you needed me. This is the space in which we are now torn apart, where I am me and you are you and we are no longer as one.

There were times I wanted to say something as we sat at the table. There were times I wanted to open up to you. But they were the times I was afraid: afraid to say something, afraid to reveal something, to 'exposé my feelings and thoughts to you. I wanted you to know my pain. I wanted you to know my desires, to know my need for you. But I have been hurt by you before. I have been hurt by you when we were as one; when we were 'open' to one another. How could I know you would not hurt me again? How could I trust you not to hurt me again?

Had I opened up to you, I would have wanted you to treat my feelings with respect. I would have also wanted you to have opened up to me. I could not talk to you. I could not do it. I thought you would see me open up. I thought you would see it as a way of tugging at me, a way of pulling at my emotions, forcing me to feel something I did not want to. Perhaps knowing how I felt would have had no effect on you. Perhaps, knowing how I felt, you would not have cared, and by not caring, you would have crushed me even further.

I was afraid that you would not give up any ground for me. That you would take advantage of my exposure in knowing how I truly felt and that somehow it would make you feel better knowing it; knowing that I might be hurt in some way, knowing that I am in as much pain as I have caused you. I wanted to give up that ground, but my fear would not let me.

I cannot say it. I cannot bring myself to say it. To say that I was wrong, to say that I was wrong in treating you the way I did. It would be like saying that it was I who hurt you, like saying that I could not live without you, that I was not strong. I hurt inside. I hurt a lot. But I cannot let you know that — it would be a sign of my weakness, it would be like saying I could not cope; you would have the upper hand, knowing that you had some power over me, the power of knowing that I am helpless without you. I feel all this and I want to say something, but I cannot. If only you had said something, something to make me feel that you regretted it, something to let me know that you might have been in the wrong, expressed some emotion to let me know that you wanted me. I wanted to hear some words from you...

But it seems that you could cope without me as I was breaking up inside.

It seems that I let you disappear. It was as if you had died. I did something I did not want to do with anyone else — let you go.

There were moments after we were separated when I wanted to cry; moments I would lie in bed with my knees held against my chest; those moments when I would hold and squeeze a pillow. These were the moments when my pain would be in my stomach. These were the moments in which I was short of breath.

There were also other times, other moments, in which I would hold a pillow; these were the times in which I was imagining you. These were the times I wanted things to be better.

I would wait hoping that you would contact me. I would wait knowing that I would not contact you. Every time there was correspondence, I would wish it was from you — my heart would get excited, starting to race, and I would come out of my mire for a few moments, hoping it was you. But when you did communicate, I would not give you an inch; I would not show my pain. I had to show that I could live without you, but inside I still wanted you.

Inside, I was angry. Inside, I was sad. Inside, I was screaming with rage. Inside, I did not know which feeling was which, but what I do know is that I would not show you my tears; they were there, running all over my heart.

These were the moments in which I would think <u>if I</u> had only done things differently. There were moments when I would think <u>if only I</u> had done things differently. There were moments when I would think <u>if only you</u> had done things differently. All I was trying to do was to make those moments perfect, perfect for me to return to you, to make it more acceptable for me.

You do not seem to understand that a whisper from you, that a tender touch, that a smile, is what compelled me to you. At every touch, at every smile, I seem to tremble inside. How could I want to lose that? How can you not understand that I had to lie?

I reached out to hold your hands across the café table. I reached out so that you could see that, whereas my words and feelings were too afraid to express themselves, this gesture could represent a bridge between my heart and yours. I had hope that you could feel the sensitivity of my hands. I had hoped that you could feel and recognise the warmth I had for you. Had you touched my hand, you would have realised that I still loved you. Had you touched my hand, you would have realised that I also needed your trust and warmth, that I wanted to feel human again. You are the only one who could have done this for me.

It seems that you may have not fully understood me. It seems that you could not have fully understood me. If you had, you would not have reached out to me across the café table. I did not want you to touch me: it would not have felt right. It would have felt as if you were like the rest of them: that you wanted to reach out and touch me because of your needs and not mine. You should not have done that. I thought you would have known. I thought you would have known that I have been hurt, that I have been hurt by you. Even though I want us to be back together, you should have known that when a woman is hurt, she will find it difficult to trust again. Despite how much I wanted to touch your hands, despite how much I have wanted so desperately to feel your gentle skin, something inside me could not let that happen. My heart wants me to, but my mind does not. Perhaps I wanted your hands to feel as I remembered them. Perhaps I did not want to associate your hands with someone I cannot trust.

Part of me regrets that I did not hold your hands. Part of me regrets that now. Trust may have been difficult, but so was seeing the back of your coat.

XIV

These Thoughts I Have

I look into the mirror and see a face I do not like. It is an expressionless face. It is a face that hides what is inside me: emotions... thoughts... words. I look into the mirror and see a distance in my eyes — a distance between myself and the world. I thought I would never see this distance again. I thought it would never appear again. It seems like time has distanced us, distanced us from when we were as one, from when there was no space between us. It is a distance that separates me from you, that detaches me from you. It is a distance that allows me to think about things, that allows me to see the thoughts rush past my eyes.

These thoughts that I have, they do not enter any space. They remain within me. They do not need to be carried by words. They cannot be carried by words: the words do not know where you are; they do not know where to find you. But my feelings and thoughts do know where to find you. They do not escape me. They are here, inside, just like you. It may have been a year since you turned your head away from me; it may have been a year since I saw you sitting in the café, but you have not left my heart or my mind.

There were times I wished you had contacted me. There were times I wished we could have met again. But you had hurt me. You had hurt me over something that seems so simple now. You had hurt me by not contacting me again. I had been waiting, waiting for that to happen. I wanted you to do that. I wanted you to take the lead, to show that you were still interested in me, to show that you still wanted me. But I suppose you were also waiting — waiting for me to contact you. I suppose you also wanted me to take the lead.

I am not sure if I could have taken the lead. I do not think you understand how it affected me. It felt as if someone had hurt me, as if they had hurt me deliberately, and as if they wanted to inflict pain *intentionally* upon me. It felt as if a chunk of me had been hacked away, as if I had lost some part of me. It felt like I had been assaulted, leaving me stunned. Everything inside me, inside my head, went blank. All I could see was you, all I could feel was pain. It was pain that prevented me from breathing, a pain that left me struggling to breathe – unable to capture the life I needed. It was a pain that was trying to suffocate me. I was struggling for my life, struggling for my existence. It was in that moment, in that instant, when all I could see was you, and you were this severe intense pain. You were the cause of this pain. You were cause of my suffocation and I had to prevent that.

In your breath was my life. In my breath was yours. But now we no longer seem to breathe as one. We no longer seem to be in unison. As you exhale, I inhale. Our hearts used to be as one also, but now yours beats as mine rests.

As your heart beats, so our child's heart would have. It seems that in the very death of our child's heart yours was jolted out of rhythm with mine. It was letting you know that as you sought to abort him you were also aborting our relationship. Now as I breathe and as my heart beats, we are no longer as one.

We are lost without one another.

I felt a sense of resentment in that space between us as we sat at the table. It was a resentment of a person in front of me who did not understand. It was a resentment of a person in front of me who did not want to understand; a resentment of someone who *intentionally* did not want to understand. It is this that hurts, knowing that you may not have wanted to understand. But I understand. I understand this because I feel this way too.

I felt a sense of uneasiness as we sat opposite one another. I felt a sense of awkwardness, something I think we were both aware of, where words would fail to escape from our lips, where we barely managed to keep our pain and hurt inside.

At the time, I sat there with a broken heart. At the time, I sat there knowing that my ideals, my hopes, were crumbling and my world collapsing. I could not say words to stop it.

We both looked at one another, knowing that the other was hurt. We did not dare admit our pain in case we revealed our true affections – in case we revealed to the other the extent of the hurt they had caused, the pain we were in.

...

There are those times I pretend I can cope. There are those times when I am with others, when those moments and instants arise — those moments and instants when we may think about each other. These are the moments when I lose awareness of my surroundings, when the voices around me seem to fade away, when everything in front of me seems to go to the back of my mind. These are the moments when I withdraw from my surroundings, being pulled in by my memories of you — those moments of truth, those instances of our feelings: the regrets and "if onlies" that constantly mar my existence; those images of yesteryear, those images of being with one another; the smiles and voices that are kept alive by my mind. It is they that detach me, in those momentary instants, from my surroundings.

In those moments, in those instants, I acknowledge what will haunt me till I die — the way we used to be. In those moments, in those instants, I know I am lost without you.

We came together like everyone does in a relationship – each with our own lives, with our own history, our own secrets, our own pain. But for a while we fused; we become one. Then after some point, after some event, something that tested us, we resorted to ourselves.

We were too absorbed in ourselves to realise what we had,

too self-absorbed to realise our relationship and, in particular, that we had one. That ourselves became priorities over our relationship. We had effectively destroyed 'us'. Destroyed 'us' because we could not move away from ourselves: I focused on me and my pain and you focused on you and your pain. The importance of us seemed to disappear into some kind of oblivion, as our angst took over.

...

When I sought their counsel, other people tried to tell me what to do. They told me so they could influence me. They said that they wanted to protect me, but deep down inside I did not want to be apart from you — I did not want this gap to exist. I longed for you to show me that you wanted me. As you turned away from me, you hurt me. You have hurt me in a way I did not think possible. But I had to protect myself; I had to listen to others even though I was screaming out for you.

...

I am sure that you did the same. I am sure that you listened to others. Those moments when we speak to them, those moments when they advise us on what to do, when they advise us on how to behave, those were the times we listened to others, the times after we separated. It was in those moments when I listened to others that I knew inside that it was those things I did not want to do. All I wanted was to get back to how it was before we were hurt; to how it was before we were wounded. All I wanted to do was to heal the pain we both felt; to wish that it never existed.

It is in those moments when I listened to them; I listened because I was hurt, because I was wounded, because I was unhappy and I wished not to be those things. I listened to those moments of advice because I believed that by doing so I could protect myself from further pain, from further hurt. Even though, deep inside, I wished I could turn back the clock to a time when we only knew of each other as one.

I listened to others because I wanted to be protected, and they also wanted to protect me. And because they wanted to protect me, they wanted me to believe in myself; they wanted me to do this by depicting you for the worse. They did this so they could lessen the anguish I would feel.

But when we do things like that, all we do is increase the pain for the other, and all the other sees is us moving further away, entrenching ourselves behind increasing layers of protection. We learn how not to show how we feel to the other, to show the other that they have not affected us, that we are strong without them. And all the other sees is that we do not want them, that we have moved on, that we move further away, that we reject them further.

It is when this happens, it is in those times of hypersensitivity, that we damage ourselves more: every little thing becomes major; every major thing is enormous; we interpret things according to our pain and do not think about the reasons for the other.

We close in and protect ourselves, tighter and tighter. We do this to prevent the pain — we do not think of how to heal it. Sometimes we think that if we try and heal it, there will be more pain; at other times, if something is as we do not expect it to be, we justify our tightening up, our closing in on ourselves. We do not seem to understand that short-term pain may help us in the long run. We do not open up, we do not want to reveal our true depth of pain, because that pain may not be comforted as we want but reinforced by a reaction that we hoped would be different.

It is strange how we miss opportunities, how time changes us. It is strange how we learn not to know one another, how our own concerns take over what should be concerns over us as a couple. It is strange how our concerns seem so big at one point – so big that we think of them as a threat to our own individual happiness. That those threats, those vulnerabilities we experience, help us learn to not know one another, help us to close in and protect ourselves, and by doing so we begin to shield ourselves from anything external to ourselves and destroy the very thing that makes us happy — each other.

There are things that we say, there are things that we do, things that we regret — things that are now in the past: little things... big things... There were things that were big in our pasts that now seem small and small things that now seem big. It is those small things that we overlooked, that we were prepared to overlook. The small things that seem so big now, seem so precious now — the gestures, the smiles, the laughter.

XV

One Four Three

After so many years, we are as one again. After all our mistakes, after all our differences, we are as one again. United, in harmony.

I have endured many years of pain without you. I have endured many years of loneliness without you. I have stayed true to you, true to us. There has never been anyone else. There will never be anyone else. I have never wanted anyone else. I will never want anyone else... Just you.

I missed you. I missed you a lot. I cannot tell you how much. I thought I had lost you. I thought I had lost you forever.

I am here now with you. I wish you had told me. I wish you had told me that you were going to go. I wish you had told me that you would leave me forever, that I would no longer see you, that you would want to leave me alone.

I think I deserved more respect than for you to not tell me, to not tell me your secret, the secret that denies me the chance

— the chance to be with you, the secret that denies the chance to be with you for a few more seconds.

I loved you. I know you loved me. I felt touched by your love... that innermost beauty. It is that innermost beauty that now tugs at me, that innermost beauty that now makes me tearful.

I am now here on my own — here with you. I have you in my arms... forever. I will never leave. I will always be yours. I will stay here... never leaving you. I will be here holding you, holding this gravestone, holding your gravestone — closing the gap between us. I will not leave you.

I know it has been a long time. I am not sure if you can hear me but I am here, here for you. I will stay here... in summer... in winter...

You are once again in my favourite place: that place which I call 'your place' — the place under my arm. When you were alive, it seemed so natural for you to be there. It is comforting to know that you are still there. It is still your place, where no one else has been. It is still your place, where no one else will ever be.

I came here to bury this watch. To let you know that I kept the gift you gave me. I kept it all these years. This watch that you gave, it stopped some time ago: it felt as if all our moments, all our time together, every second we spent with one another, had ended. But I had it repaired. I had it repaired so that I could see the seconds in action again, so that I could re-live our moments together.

But soon after, the watch stopped again. Those seconds that had survived were like every heartbeat you and I shared. Those seconds may have passed but the heartbeats have continued. I wanted you to know that whilst time had stopped, my heart did not.

I just want to say that these years that have passed... have been lonely.

Even though it was I who wanted to separate, even though I had decided that, it was in that moment when I expressed those nine words to you that I felt a gap between us. It felt as if my very being, my body, every cell which exists in my body, was being torn apart, being ripped apart — it was so painful, it hurt so much. How can I ever express to you the effect of breaking the trust I felt? It felt as if I had been wounded, as if I had been mortally wounded. It was as if something was eating me inside. It felt as if I had to cut off my right arm just to save myself.

Even now, after having every cell torn apart, after the ripping of my heart, of my mind, of my body, of my soul, even after that, there is a part of you in me. As I am you, you are me, we are as one — inseparable, and I love you so.

I wish I had a chance to say things to you, things that I wanted to say, things that I needed to say. We left one another not on good terms. We left one another knowing that we did not want to, yet feeling that we had to. As the space between us grew, it stretched and tore the bond we had; our movement apart cut its way through our closeness. I think, at the time, all we felt were the cuts and tears — we could not see ourselves. The pain seemed to be too immediate to notice one another. The pain was too immediate to notice 'us'. We were right for each other.

For many months and years, you were in my heart and in my mind. But as the cuts and pain ebbed away, my memories of 'us' grew in strength. You were the other person I had lost. You were the other half of me. You were my life.

I knew something was wrong – I knew. I knew something had happened to you; I felt it in my soul. I felt something, I felt something that disturbed me; it seemed like a ripple disturbing still waters. It was then that those disturbed waters led me to look for you. They led me to your son.

I met your son. He is a nice man. He is a good man. You should be very proud. He took me in his counsel.

I told him that I was an old friend. I told him that I had not seen you for some time. I showed him a picture of you, a picture that I still carry in my breast pocket. He, in return, showed me a picture of you. I could see what you looked like. After so many years I saw what you looked like. And even though it has been many... many years — you looked like the first day I met you. You were beautiful. You *are* beautiful.

I think your son saw how moved I was by your picture. I think he must have known we were good friends, that we must have been close to one another. He looked at me. He looked at me in his sorrow and asked me about something he did not understand. He told me he needed to understand something about his mother. He told me that you had been cutting yourself, that you must have been doing this for some time. And that your death was due to an infection, an infection that was from one of your cuts. He told me that they were small cuts. He told me that there were lots of small cuts. He told me that the doctor had said there were a hundred and forty-three cuts. One hundred and forty-three... One... four... three... one four three.

He said he could not understand. He said he could also not understand why you had cut yourself there. I asked him to show me. He moved his hands from one side of his abdomen to the other. It was the part of the abdomen, just below where the cord is that sustains your life when one is in the birth chamber. But he kept making his hand movements from the place and side where I had my scar.

Is he my son? Is he? Is he what ties us together? He would have been born several months after we separated. Last time we met, we met in the café. You were sitting down. I could not have seen if you were with child. I think he could be my son. I will never know. It's a pity... Pity, because I have no children of my own and the one I think I have I know nothing of.

All this because of a lie.

How much of an effect does a lie have? Who can assess? Who can assess this? Perhaps the tears that are wept indicate the true impact of a lie. Perhaps the length of the trail of tears that are wept indicate how long it lasts: one tear — a day, two — a month, another — a year...

These tears that trickle from my heart, they do not stop. I have lost count of the number of times it has wept. It now weeps for the memory of a lie. The lie itself has passed, but my heart holds onto the emotions, holding onto you.

I wake up at times, wanting to speak these words: 'Dear Heart, why have you forsaken me?' But my heart cannot hear — I left her a long time ago, she has now died. You are my heart, darling. You can no longer hear. Why did you have to die?

I miss you so much. How I miss you! The pain was there and you were not. I held a pillow. I held you in my arms. I held you tightly but it was still there — the pain.

I sometimes imagine your lips. I try to remember the times you kissed me. I try to remember your soft tenderness pressing upon mine. I imagine your lips gently kissing my heart: kissing to make it better; kissing to heal it. I imagine this.

I also imagine my eyes closing in relief, knowing that your lips have touched my heart, knowing that I am no longer lonely.

There were words I wanted to say to you. There were words I wanted you to hear. 'Sorry' was one of them. 'Love' was another. But time passes by and all I have is regrets. My skin has aged, my hair has greyed, my teeth have fallen out, but my memory remains youthful.

You are still with me. You are still here — in my heart.

These tears that I have, they are for you. I hope they fall onto your grave. I hope they nourish this earth around you, so that I can be consumed by it, so that I can lie next to you, so that I can see your face again, so that I can see these tears run across your cheeks, and so that I can see your smile — that smile you showed me every morning when we were together, when we were as one. I want to be a part of the earth that is beside you. I want to be here for the rest of my life. To close that gap that is now between us. Maybe my body could merge with yours. You... I... Us... as one.

I have loved you. I will always love you from the bottom of my heart. I have given you my heart and now I am in need of yours.

You are my first love. You are my only love. I want to die here with you, die with you in my arms and with my hand resting upon your abdomen.

...

I refuse to look at us, to look at what we had, to look at our lives together with any misgivings. I may have had regrets, but none were about you, they were about what had happened. I refuse to say, just because of the pain, just because of the unhappiness of our separation, I refuse to say I wish it never happened.

There was a reason why we were together. I had known you for a long time; I had known you for most of my adult life when we had parted. I had known and loved you for that time. And in that time I had also changed; I had changed because of you. You had provided me with things that no one else had: you let me know what joy was, you taught me how to smile, you let me know what it was to be human. How could I regret that? How could I allow myself to regret that?

Those last few months when we were together, those months in which the space between us was growing, those were the times which were stressful, those were the times of tension. But those few months did not make up our life together; they will not constitute or taint the way I feel about you.

You were a part of me. We were as one. We were *our* relationship and not two separate people within a relationship. At times it was too painful to love you... You meant so much. Every little thing that you said or did formed a part of me — when you were in pain, I was in pain. I did not like seeing you disheartened. I did not like seeing you cry. I wanted to help. I wanted to protect you. I wanted to rescue you from your unhappiness when it was there. I wanted to hold you, to let you know that you were safe.

Right now, I need to hold you. I need to hold that part of me that was you, that part that was literally half of me — the part of me that I wanted to make happy, that part that I wanted to protect, a half that was once mine. Me, you — as one.

You were the other half of me. My twin half: the half that had parted; the half that had died; my twin that had died. But I have memories, memories of you — my other half. I have memories of 'us'.

Do you remember the times when we were together, the times when we were as one? When there was no gap between us? Do you remember the times when we smiled at one another, when we laughed together? Do you remember those times? They were good times. Times that are forever forged into my heart, times that still keep beating.

Do you remember that time? Do you remember that time when I spilled some drink on myself? Do you remember that time? You know, that time when we were going to K_____, that time when I was trying to open a bottle of water. As I did, some of the water spilled out onto me and I did not notice. Do you remember? Do you remember when you saw my face when I realised what had happened? You laughed at me. You laughed at me because you thought I was like a little baby. You know that face – that face when a baby does not know something has happened but then he realises that something belonging to him has been 'ruined'. You know that face. That face just before a baby starts to cry. You said that I had that look on me – that I realised that something of mine was 'ruined'. Do you remember that? You laughed. I remember it. I remember that you laughed so much. You laughed so much after seeing how I reacted to it.

I remember you bending over with laughter. It was then that I said something to you that made you laugh even more. It was the most I had seen you laughing. Do you remember that time when you laughed and your beautiful teeth showed? Do you remember? I remember. I remember that you had beautiful teeth and a beautiful smile. I remember that your teeth were showing so much that I held my hand out in front of your mouth. I held my hand there and told you, in jest, because of your hearty laughter, that I held my hand out in front of your mouth to ensure that your teeth would not fall out. Do you remember? I remember. I remember because you could not stop laughing for a long time. You could not stop laughing for a long time after what I said. I remember because we both knew you had a beautiful smile and beautiful teeth. Do you remember it? Do you remember that time when you laughed so much that your teeth almost fell out? Do you remember that time?

I remember those times. I remember them and others. I remember them because they were not the big grand gestures of romance. I remember them because they were *our* gestures of romance. It was our laughter, in our situations, in our moments — it was our romance.

I remember your smile, your beautiful smile. I will always remember that.

I remember the time I was in hospital. That time I was in hospital and I was waking up after the anaesthesia. I remember it. I remember that my first sight, upon waking, was of you. I was drowsy, but you were there. Do you remember it? I remember it because it was important for me to know that the person I loved was there for me.

I remember your face. I remember it. I was barely awake. It was on your face that I saw your concern. It was on your face that I saw your pain. It was on your face that I saw your love for me.

I remember that just before I fell back to sleep you kissed me. You did not think that I would remember that, but I did. I always have. I was and have been touched by that gesture – knowing that you were there for me whilst I was ill. To have known in your kiss all the love, care and concern that you had for me.

I remember that.

I remember that when I was fully awake, I saw your smile. I remember seeing your smile — it meant everything to me.

I remember the times when you used to wake me up early. You used to wake me up even though you knew I did not like waking up early. You would curl up on top of me. You would rest your head on my chest. I remember that. I remember you curling up on top of me and resting your head upon my chest. I remember that as I opened my eyes you would look up and smile at me. I remember those times. They were beautiful times.

It was not just those times, when you used to wake me up

early, it was all those times; it was all those mornings which I remember. It was when I woke up and I would see you. I would see you in that instant, in that moment, when I looked beside me as I woke up, seeing you lying next to me, seeing your smile.

I remember your smile, your beautiful smile. I will always remember that.

Author's Note

Malady began as a meditation on relationships: how we, as humans, destroy what is of most value to us. Upon reflection, we can see how our behaviours might have prevented the very thing we ruin. The implosion in *Malady* gestates from a lie — something corrosive that enters a relationship and which may never leave it.

To establish the lie, I wanted something that was symbolic of destruction. What more emotive subject can there be than the loss of a child? Inevitably, the lie would involve either the question of parentage or the concealment of an abortion/miscarriage. Both form the basis of betrayal.

In researching another project about twins, the premise of *Malady* came to fruition in its entirety. I tried to liken the 'special' bonding of identical twins with the bonding of a couple in a relationship. The research led me to the reality of twin loss - not just the adult or childhood experience of twin loss, but also intrauterine twin loss. Here I made the connection with abortions, i.e. the womb.

I also used a premise, not based on the research, that

intrauterine twin loss survivors need to find a compensatory partner. Though this, in itself, was not sufficient to move forward with the project, I needed to establish a connection between a surviving twin and a survivor's need to undertake an abortion as an adult. Although I found the concept of a prenatal 'ghost twin' intriguing, I elected to use the condition called 'Twin To Twin Transfusion Syndrome' (TTTS). Here, the blood supply is greater to one twin than the other, through placental differentiations. The smaller twin may also have a smaller umbilical or blood supply. There are complications that can occur but I was interested in the condition as an idea for this fiction: that the diversion of blood from one person to another can cause death.

There are also areas in psychology that refer to birth trauma and intrauterine experience. I felt that all these ideas were sufficient to create a story.

To establish the lie, the intentionality of the deception had to be sufficient to cause a fracture in a relationship. Whilst the abortion was what was concealed, the miscarriage was the tool to deceive. The intention to deceive using such an emotive topic would make a separation certain.

The reader may notice that in these notes, the key elements are overwhelmingly female-oriented. One could make the assumption that the story is primarily *her* story. Indeed, the destruction of the child and the subsequent breakdown of the relationship is literally *her* story: the subversion of a woman as creator and nurturer to that of a destroyer. Some of these destructive elements can be seen in the Appendix, where I have included some draft notes which I felt I was unable to use in *Malady*. However, I wanted to continue with the subversive theme and have the male character as the 'victim' in the relationship.

His story was never going to be as 'glamorous' in the eyes of the world. The world can relate to children and babies but not necessarily to the inner turmoil of an individual: children being universal as compared to inner anxiety. But his story had to be equally important in the construction of the relationship.

I elected to use *selective mutism* for various reasons; primarily, the inability to speak through high levels of anxiety in specific situations and also, by connection, the concept of trust within a relationship. This would also provide a link to the common perception that men, perhaps, have difficulty in expressing themselves as adults.

However, there may have been difficulty in relating to an anxiety that very few people have and, for all intents and purposes, is innate. People may understand anxiety, but they may not understand an innate fear. As such, I had to put a cause to the anxiety that could bridge people's comprehension. And so the innate fear of speaking became the fear of speaking in case people die. A slight shift but, nevertheless, everyone can understand the consequences of an action.

Strangely, the chapter 'Afraid to Speak' is quite verbose. However, the essence of the chapter was to address the difficulty in expressing emotions, attempting a systematic breakdown as to why the male character had difficulty revealing emotions: the initial fear, the fear in speaking and the subsequent fear of having spoken.

Obviously, the fear and trust of others was to be central to the separation. This may not be as strong as the female story, but it is a strong reason within the relationship. The heart of the matter, then, is whether a relationship is about two individuals or whether it should be seen as one unit.

Furthermore, I try to infer that in relationships people tend to retreat into themselves. Here, the two characters resort to their respective pathological pasts, or respond at times of stress with earlier learnt patterns of behaviour. Thus in times of tension, people begin to see the tension and not the reasons why they happen to be with their partner in the first place. Is this a survival instinct? Does our humanity prevent us from being content?

'Talking in her Ear' was difficult to write in a dialogue-only manuscript. Did I really want the moans and groans in the dialogue format, together with the Bad Sex Award? I resolved it by the use of a description of one character's desire being explained to the other. As *Malady* was about the description of thoughts and emotions, so the issue of sex had to be descriptive in its action. It therefore had to be somewhat graphic. It then led me to also have a detailed description of an abortion. Thus sex and death would be presented equally graphically.

Finally, it may be noted that I use some strong existential themes: fear, death, loneliness and anxiety. Whilst I do not use them in their absolute philosophical sense, i.e. as givens to our lives, I have tried to incorporate them into an individual's pathological past. This was primarily to aid in understanding these themes. Not entirely a happy concoction, but indicative of a doomed relationship.

Appendix

Below are some notes, left in draft, which I felt I was unable to use in *Malady*. You will be able to see that after undertaking the research and looking at images of aborted foetuses, heightened emotions arose, such that they led me to question whether abortion was compatible with humanity.

Although emotions were high, I was trying to convey them in the male character. However, they became too political and some semblances of a theory were emerging, which was ultimately beyond the purpose of *Malady*.

[DRAFT]

1.

It is there, where our children die. It is there, in your womanhood. They die in that chamber of yours. When they leave me they are alive. When they are in you they die. Your sex, your womanhood... is their place of death.

And when one does survive, when you are with child, you forget about the rest. You say you will love a child, but you do so to avoid guilt over the death of the others to avoid responsibility for their deaths.

But you, you, when you were eventually with child, you chose to destroy that one. It happens there, in your womanhood, it happens there in that chamber of death. As you are a 'woman', as you are 'you' you are full of death and you care not for me.

2.

It is women, it is women who prevent and destroy life. Even when you take those contraceptives, when you take those female hormones — it is about the non-existence of life.

You are not satisfied by the death of all those that left me. You show no compassion, no compunction for the one that survived. You do what you women do best — exercise your chamber of death.

3.

Viable! Viable! A dead body is not viable, but do you see me dismembering it? If I did, you would think that I was a sick man.

4.

All I can see in my mind is a perfect baby. All I can see in my mind is an image of our child dismembered, its limbs apart... its head smashed. And because I cannot get this image out of my head, that image makes me feel like... Like you are some kind of murderer. This thought, this thought, it just will not go away. Every time I look at you, I see a dismembered child. I cannot look at you in the same way anymore.

Acknowledgements

The following materials were used as background reading and I wish to thank the authors for their inspiration.

Books:

Burke, Theresa & Reardon, David C (2007) *Forbidden Grief: The unspoken pain of abortion*. Illinois: Acorn Books

Cline, Tony and Baldwin, Sylvia (2005) *Selective Mutism in Children*. Second Edition. London: Whurr Publishers Ltd

Don, Andrews (2005) *Fathers Feel Too*. London: Bosun Publications (for SANDS)

Condon, Guy and Hazard, David (2001) *Fatherhood Aborted: The Profound Effects of Abortion on Men*. Illinois,USA: Tyndale

Kohner, Nancy and Henley, Alix (2001) *When a Baby Dies: The Experience of Late Miscarriage, Stillbirth and Neonatal Death*. Revised Edition. London: Routledge.

McHolm, Angel E., Cunningham, Charles E. and Vanier, Melanie K. (2005) *Helping Your Child with Selective Mutism: Practical Steps to Overcome a Fear of Speaking.* Oakland, CA.: New Harbinger Publications, Inc.

Moulder, Christine (2001) *Miscarriage: Women's Experience and Needs.* London: Routledge.

Shostak, A. B., McLouth, G & Seng, Lynn (1984) *Men and Abortion: Lessons, Losses and Love.* New York: Praeger Scientific.

Woodward, Joan (1999) *The Lone Twin: Understanding Twin Bereavement and Loss.* London: Free Association Books

Internet Information

Warning: websites marked with an asterisks (*) have graphic illustrations of an abortion and should be viewed with caution

Abortion Education website: *
http://www.abortioneducation.org/ae/WhatHappens/What 03.htm

Abortion Facts website:
http://www.abortionfacts.com/

Everybody website – information about miscarriage:
http://www.everybody.co.nz/page-981ecffe-712a-4d21-b559-baff3abd2de2.aspx

Fatherhood Forever website:
http://www.fatherhoodforever.org/

Life website: *
http://www.life.org.nz/abortion/aboutabortion/methods/

Men and Abortion:
http://www.menandabortion.info/index.html

Miscarriage Association:
http://www.miscarriageassociation.org.uk/

SMIRA – Select Mutism and Research Association:
http://www.selectivemutism.co.uk/

Selective Mutism Organisation:
http://www.selectivemutism.org/

The UK Twin To Twin Transfusion Syndrome Association:
http://www.twin2twin.org/

These websites were last visited on 30 January 2010.

Internet Help Websites:

The following websites were not used as background material, but are given should readers be affected by what they have read:

CRUSE Bereavement Care:
http://www.crusebereavementcare.org.uk/

SANDS (Stillbirth and Neonatal Death Society):
http://www.uk-sands.org/

Twinless Twins Support Group International:
http://www.twinlesstwins.org/

Twins UK, a website for and about twins. It has some references to twin loss:
http://www.twinsuk.co.uk/index.php

These websites were last visited on 30 January 2010.